Acclaim for Kimberla Lawson Roby's Novels

SECRET OBSESSION

"The lengths Paige goes to...sure keep the pages turning...Fans of Roby's Curtis Black novels will find this one true to form."

—*Booklist*

"[A] juicy read!"

—*Essence*

"*New York Times* bestselling author Kimberla Lawson Roby has a knack for writing suspenseful, page-turning stories, and her latest novel, SECRET OBSESSION, is no different...A must-read for fiction thriller fans."

—TheRoot.com

"The kind of novel I wish more authors would write...addictive."
—ChickLitReviewsandNews.com

LOVE, HONOR, AND BETRAY

"Lively, action-packed, and full of sassy sensuality...Roby once again has created a story that grabs the reader's attention and holds it in her grip until the very end."

—*Las Vegas Review Journal*

Secret Obsession

Also by Kimberla Lawson Roby

Shalonda,

Secret Obsession

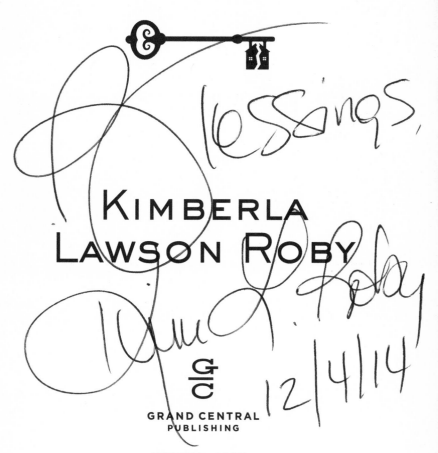

Blessings,

KIMBERLA
LAWSON ROBY

Kim L. Roby

12/4/14

GRAND CENTRAL
PUBLISHING

NEW YORK   BOSTON

Copyright © 2011 by Kimberla Lawson Roby

Grand Central Publishing
Hachette Book Group
237 Park Avenue
New York, NY 10017

www.HachetteBookGroup.com

Printed in the United States of America

RRD-C

Originally published in hardcover by Grand Central Publishing.

First Trade Edition: August 2012

10 9 8 7 6 5 4 3 2 1

Grand Central Publishing is a division of Hachette Book Group, Inc.

The Grand Central Publishing name and logo is a trademark of Hachette Book Group, Inc.

The Hachette Speakers Bureau provides a wide range of authors for speaking events. To find out more, go to www.hachettespeakersbureau.com or call (866) 376-6591.

The publisher is not responsible for websites (or their content) that are not owned by the publisher.

The Library of Congress has cataloged the hardcover edition as follows:

Roby, Kimberla Lawson.
Secret obsession / Kimberla Lawson Roby. — 1st ed.
p. cm.
ISBN 978-0-446-57242-2
1. African American women—Fiction. I. Title.
PS3568.O3189S43 2011
813'.54—dc22

2011003698

ISBN 978-0-446-57241-5 (pbk.)

For Kathy Vigna

My first professional mentor.
A woman I've always admired.
The woman I've always looked up to in the business world.
The best boss I ever had.

Acknowledgments

First, I thank God for guiding and protecting my family and me and for continuing to bless us in every way. Without You, nothing would be possible, and I am forever grateful.

To my heart and joy—my husband, Will. I love you with everything in me. Your love has remained unconditional since the very beginning, and I thank God for you every day of my life.

I also want to thank my wonderful family members whom I love so, so much. Your unwavering support means everything: my brothers, Willie Jr. and Michael Stapleton; my stepson and daughter-in-law, Trenod and Tasha Vines-Roby; my aunts and uncles, Clifton and Vernell Tennin, Ben Tennin, Luther Tennin, Charlie and Mary Beasley, Earl and Fannie Haley-Rome, Ada Tennin, James Tennin, and Ollie Tennin; all of my cousins, sisters-in-law, and brothers-in-law (way too many to name individually but you all know who you are!); my girls of girls who are more like blood sisters, Kelli Bullard, Lori Thurman, and Janell Green; and the wonderful mothers of my nieces and nephews, Karen Young, Danetta Taylor, and April Farris.

Much love and many thanks to my spiritual mother, Dr. Betty Price; my author friends, Patricia Haley (also my first cousin!), Victoria Christopher Murray, Trisha R. Thomas, Trice Hickman,

Eric Jerome Dickey, Eric Pete, Mary Morrison, ReShonda Tate Billingsley, and Curtis Bunn, to name just a few.

To my assistant, Connie Dettman: you are simply the best, and I'm not sure how I would manage without you. Thank you for being so kind and for all you do. I also want to say a special thanks to my freelance publicist, Shandra Hill Smith, my website developer and e-card/advertisement designer, Luke Lefevre, and my newsletter graphic designer and programmer, Pamela Walker-Williams. You guys are beyond amazing!

Then, to all of the wonderful folks at Grand Central Publishing. You are each an author's dream, and I am so blessed to be working with such a talented and caring team. My editor-in-chief/editor, Beth de Guzman; my manuscript editor, Selina McLemore; assistant editor, Latoya Smith; my publisher, Jamie Raab; my publicity director, Linda Duggins; associate publicist, Samantha Kelly; my online marketing gurus Anna Balasi and Brad Parsons; my production editor, Dorothea Halliday; my art director, Elizabeth Connor; the entire sales force, the entire marketing team, and everyone else at Hachette/GCP who works so hard on each of my titles. Thanks a million for everything.

To all the book clubs nationwide that choose my work as their monthly selection, to all the bookstores that sell my work to the masses, and to all the radio and TV producers, talk show hosts, anchors, and newspaper and magazine editors/writers who review or feature my novels. Thank you for all your support.

And finally to the most important people of all—the folks who allow me to do what I love and who are kind enough to support me with every single book release: my fabulous readers. From the bottom of my heart, I say thank you.

With all my love and many blessings,
Kimberla Lawson Roby

Prologue

Paige Donahue glanced around the elegant dining room and literally wanted to die. She hated visiting her sister, she hated all that Camille had been blessed with, and most important, she hated *her*. In fact, she always had, ever since childhood, thanks to the way their parents had doted on Camille and treated her like she was just a bit more precious. They'd gone out of their way, confirming the idea that Camille was the better daughter, their golden child so to speak, and that Paige was the very least of their worries. They'd even as much as told Paige this very thing on several different occasions—maybe not directly, of course, but their actions had made their feelings dreadfully clear. Such as the time when she'd turned sixteen and they'd told her how they simply couldn't afford to give her the same pricey sweet-sixteen party they'd given Camille just two years before, since they now had to save all their money for Camille's graduation gala. Worse, they'd never even apologized for it and had merely expected Paige to accept their decision. And it was the same situation when they'd purchased Camille that brand-new SUV right before she left for college but had convinced Paige that there was nothing wrong with driving her sister's hand-me-down, ten-year-old Camry when she graduated—that is, since Paige would *only* be traveling ten miles down the road to a junior college. It was true that Camille had done much better than Paige in high school, and yes, Camille had practically breezed through Marquette with honors, and right after had immediately been hired by one of Chicago's top advertising firms. But had that given George and Maxine Donahue the right to treat their younger daughter like she didn't matter? Had it been okay for them to boast about Camille's high accomplishments to anyone who would listen and then constantly compare those accomplishments to all that Paige had failed at? Had it been okay for them to insist that maybe if Paige had been just a tad more like Camille, they'd have been a lot prouder of her?

Even today, Paige still hadn't forgiven them, doubted she ever would, and pretty much kept her distance. From her parents, anyway, because when it came to Camille, Paige had always visited her regularly and never let on how she truly felt about her—not once. They did everything sisters should do together, and Paige went out of her way to let Camille know that she loved her and would give her life for her if she had to. She'd done all of this for years because she needed her sister to love and trust her completely. She needed her to trust her so much that she would never suspect what was coming. Paige had denied herself for fifteen agonizing years, partly because she didn't want to hurt Crystal and PJ, her adorable niece and nephew, but as of a few months ago, they'd turned ten and twelve, respectively—meaning they were older and wiser and would handle things a lot better now. They would still be hurt, that much she knew for sure, but not devastated.

Paige smiled at her sister, then at her flawless-looking brother-in-law, Pierce, and then at the children. She lifted one of the freshly baked dinner rolls from the basket, set it back onto the table, and pretended she couldn't be happier.

"So, how's business this month?" Camille asked Paige, referring to the public relations firm Paige had founded shortly after being laid off from her previous job.

"Not bad. I'm still working with my three ongoing clients, and I just contracted two short-term clients a couple of days ago."

"That's really great, sis," Camille said, and Paige could tell Camille was genuinely happy for her. Too bad Paige could barely stand the sight of *her*—too bad Paige envied everything about her sister, including her beautiful, extremely thick, off-black shoulder-length hair and her ridiculously toned five-foot-ten-inch frame. Even sitting down, there was no mistaking how statuesque and attractive Camille was, and suddenly Paige felt ill, so much so that she wanted to leave. But she knew escaping the situation wouldn't help her, and she pulled herself together.

"I think it's wonderful how you were able to start your own business and find so much success with it," Pierce said. "Truly impressive."

"Why, thank you." Paige wanted to hug him.

Pierce was an honestly good man who had always been very kind to her, and she loved him for it. He was one of the best men she knew, and while he'd graduated at the top of his MBA class sixteen years ago and was now a top bank executive earning well into the mid–six figures, he treated her as an equal. He never talked down to her the way her parents did, and she appreciated that. She appreciated everything about him and had felt this way ever since first laying eyes on him. As a matter of fact, it seemed only days ago when Camille had finally decided to bring Pierce to their parents' home for dinner. He'd been the perfect gentleman, and Paige had known immediately that Camille wasn't about to let him get away. So there was no surprise when the two of them had announced their engagement only three months later and had begun planning the wedding of the century. Their parents had even taken out a sizable home equity loan, used a portion of their savings, and their mother had acted as though she'd been the one who was actually getting married. She'd been so excited about her first daughter tying the knot, and to Paige's great disappointment, Camille and Pierce's wedding had ended up being the most talked-about nuptials in Covington Park—the south suburb of Chicago where Paige and Camille had grown up and where they all still resided. Paige also remembered how miserable she'd been, standing next to her sister, serving as her maid of honor, and how she'd wished it was her who'd met the perfect man and was going to live happily ever after.

But the longer Paige sat reminiscing about her overall relationship with her sister and how terribly her parents had treated her, the more certain she was of her decision. She was going to take what rightly should have been hers from the very beginning: her brother-in-law, Pierce Montgomery. She would take what belonged to her, which wouldn't be very difficult, considering how there had always been an obvious attraction between the two of them—Paige may not have been as tall as Camille, but she'd been told on more than a number of occasions that she was beautiful. So, yes, things would work out just the way they were supposed to, and soon, Pierce would realize he'd fallen in love with the wrong sister. Soon, Pierce would fall madly in love with Paige, he would ask his darling wife for a divorce, and he and Paige would marry at a lovely resort in the Caribbean. They would become husband and wife the way God intended. Paige knew this because she'd plotted a very clever plan.

Chapter 1

One Week Later

$\mathcal{P}$aige smiled at Owen Richardson, her boyfriend of one year, and wondered how she'd tolerated him for so long. But she knew why. He worshiped the ground she walked on, and the sex between them could sometimes be out of this world. Still, he was no Pierce Montgomery. He wasn't even half the man her brother-in-law was, not when you compared their looks, charisma, and personality, and Owen's financial situation had never sat well with her either. Of course, there was no denying that he did earn a great salary as a fireman, but he didn't bring in nearly enough money to excite Paige. He didn't make the kind of money that would keep her satisfied or afford her a much more glamorous home— something much better than the average-looking one she lived in currently.

Owen took a bite of the chicken quesadilla they'd just had delivered and then drank a sip of soda. "Such a great movie, isn't it, baby?"

"Yeah, it really is," Paige said, referring to *The Blind Side*, which she'd already seen with a friend when it was first released at the theater and also two other times on one of the pay channels.

"I just love how the Tuohys took in Michael Oher, loved him like he was their own child, and also made sure he got a great education. Not to mention, you could tell he'd been a great kid all along. Just needed someone to guide and care about him."

"Yeah, that really was sweet of them," Paige said, barely paying Owen any attention because she was now daydreaming about Pierce—wondering what he was doing and whether he was thinking of her as well. Oh how desperately she wanted to be with him and couldn't wait to begin implementing the fabulous strategy she'd come up with. Her plan was absolutely brilliant, and she couldn't help smiling when she thought about the future outcome. Just visualizing the two of them together forever made her tingly all over.

"Paige!" she heard Owen yelling. "Have you heard a word I said?"

"What? Of course I have."

"Then why did I have to call your name three different times before you answered? I mean, what are you so preoccupied about?"

"Nothing."

"It doesn't seem like nothing to me."

"You're just paranoid."

"Yeah, whatever," he said, turning back toward the television with an annoyed look on his face.

Paige knew he hadn't believed her and now had a slight attitude, but in truth, she couldn't have cared less.

They watched another twenty minutes of the movie, and then out of nowhere Owen's face softened and he got serious. He muted the volume on the remote and turned his body completely toward her. Paige wondered what this was all about.

"You know," he said, "I've been debating whether to have this discussion with you for a good while now, but for some reason, tonight feels right. We just made the most passionate love, and I've never been more sure about our relationship."

Paige wasn't sure she liked where this conversation was headed and didn't say anything.

"You know I love you, right?" he said, continuing.

"Yeah, I guess."

"I love you more than anything in this world."

Paige fell silent again, and when Owen moved from the sofa and down to the floor on one knee, her heart dropped. He positioned himself directly in front of her and then pulled out a tiny royal blue velvet box. "Paige Donahue, will you marry me?"

Paige was taken aback and still had no words to speak. She tried answering him, or at least to make some sort of comment, but she couldn't.

"Sweetheart, I know we haven't spoken much about marriage, but I don't think my feelings about you have ever been a secret. I love you and want to spend the rest of my life with you, so how about it? Will you do me the great honor of becoming my wife?"

"I . . . I . . . Look, Owen," she finally said. "This is truly very kind of you, but I'm sorry to say that I'm not ready for marriage."

Owen stared at her, clearly hurt by her rejection. "But why?"

"Because I'm just not."

"So does this mean you don't love me?"

"No. It doesn't mean that at all, but I have to be honest. I love you, but I'm not *in* love with you."

Owen sighed deeply, got to his feet, and sat back down on the sofa. Paige saw how devastated, heartbroken, and confused he was, but there was nothing she could do about it.

"I'm really sorry," she said innocently.

Owen set the tiny box down on the glass coffee table. "Wow," he said, shaking his head. "I feel like a complete fool. Especially, since you've been telling me for months that you *did* love me."

"That's because I do. But not in the way a woman should love a man when she's ready to marry him."

Owen looked at her, noticeably perturbed. "Well, Paige, if you weren't in love with me and you've known that you weren't all this time, then why have you been allowing me to pay half of your car note every month and take you shopping in stores I really couldn't afford? Not to mention the cash I gave you from almost every paycheck."

"I don't get what you mean," she said, acting as though she didn't understand what he was saying.

"You know exactly what I mean. Why did you use me the way you did?"

Paige raised her eyebrows, now losing patience with him. "Look, Owen. I never forced you to do any of those things. You helped with my car payment and bought nice things for me all on your own."

Owen folded his arms. "So, not once did you hint around about how tough things were for you or how hard it was paying all your bills? Not once did you tell me you were experiencing a slow period with clients and that you didn't know what you were going to do?"

Paige looked away from him, knowing she *had* hinted a few times about her eight-hundred-dollar Lexus car payment on purpose and how she had also lured him into high-end department stores, only to express how much she loved a certain dress or handbag. She'd told him how she wished she could buy some of those things but just couldn't afford it. She'd done this because she'd learned early on that Owen did care a lot for her and wanted her to be happy. She'd discovered how compassionate he was, and, right or wrong, she'd preyed on his sympathy every chance she'd gotten. Now, though, she wanted nothing to do with the idea of marrying him and hoped he would eventually understand that.

"So, what does this mean for us?" he asked, still angry. "I mean,

do you think you'll ever be in love with me? Will you ever want
to become my wife?"

Paige hesitated for a few seconds, then said, "No. I'm sorry, but
I just don't see that happening."

"Wow," he said.

Paige placed her hand on the side of his arm. "I really am
sorry."

Owen grabbed his jeans and sweater from the back of the sofa
and slipped them on. "I don't know when I've ever been more disappointed or pissed off. But hey, I guess it is what it is."

"I never meant to hurt you, Owen. I never meant for things to
turn out this way," she said, because she honestly hadn't planned
on their relationship ending so soon. Although, deep down, she
had to admit that she wasn't terribly bothered by it, because once
she and Pierce finally got together, she would have had to end
things with Owen anyhow. She would have had to notify him
abruptly, and that scenario might have made things worse.

Owen pulled on his leather jacket and walked toward the front
door, and Paige followed behind him.

"I know I've apologized, but I just want to say again how sorry
I am."

"I'll see you later, Paige," he said, opening the door.

"Owen, I know you're upset right now, but I do hope we can
still be friends."

Owen walked out of the condo and never looked back at her.

Paige watched him stroll toward the driveway and get into
his car. She truly was very sorry, but she could never love him
the way he wanted her to, so there was no sense delaying the inevitable. Surprisingly, though, she did feel a little sad and felt bad
for Owen, but she had to move on. What she had to do now was
focus on more critical matters—her brother-in-law—and this, of
course, made her smile again. The whole idea of it all lifted her

spirits and made her want to take a shower and turn in early. That way she would have even longer to dream about her future husband.

Yes, life was going to be just grand once Paige became the next Mrs. Pierce Montgomery—something that would happen a lot sooner than anyone could imagine.

Chapter 2

*G*lass shattered, and Paige's eyes popped wide open. Then she heard a loud thud and looked over at the clock. But as soon as she did, the intruder rushed into the bedroom. She quickly grabbed her cordless phone, but the tall muscular man snatched it away from her and slammed it against the wall.

The moonlight shone through Paige's window, and she could now see part of his face. "Are you absolutely sure you want to go through with this?" the man asked.

"I've never been more sure about anything."

At first the man hesitated, but then he grabbed both her legs and dragged her closer to him.

Paige squirmed to the other side of the bed, but when he pulled her back, he slapped her so brutally she saw stars.

"That's it," she said, moaning in pain. "But harder."

The man sighed but did as he was told. He beat her repeatedly with both his fists, and Paige broke into real tears.

Next, the man pulled out a gun and struck her across the face with it. He struck her three different times, and Paige bellowed out in sheer agony.

The man backed away from her. "Paige, please. I just can't do this."

"Yes you can!" she exclaimed. "You promised me you would. Now come on!"

The intruder sighed again, set his gun down on the nightstand, and savagely ripped Paige's nightgown apart. Then he lunged on top of her, and the two of them struggled like longtime enemies.

At the same time, though, Paige hoped Pierce would appreciate the fact that she'd literally had to concoct this whole rape scheme just so they could be together. She hadn't wanted to take things this far, having to endure such excruciating and violent physical pain, but it was a sacrifice she'd been fully willing to make. She'd done so because she knew it was all going to be very much worth her while in the end—she knew when it was all said and done, Pierce would thank her profusely and would be glad to know she was the kind of woman who was willing to do anything. Anything at all to be with him.

Chapter 3

Detectives and police officers were scattered everywhere. Outside the house, inside Paige's bedroom, inside the kitchen, and also in the living room where Paige was sitting now, bawling hysterically and lying in Camille's arms. Pierce was standing nearby, too, right next to her parents, George and Maxine, and Paige was glad she'd dialed Camille immediately after calling 911.

"I'm so, so sorry," Camille said to her sister, crying along with her.

Paige sniffled and held Camille even tighter but slightly pulled her face away from her sister's chest because of all the pain. Her face was severely swollen, her lower lip was busted, and her right eye was slightly closed as well.

"I just don't see how something like this could happen," Maxine finally said. "And why on earth wasn't your security system armed?"

Paige raised her head up and frowned. "Mom, is that all you care about? An alarm system and how I forgot to set it?"

"No, but with all the crime that goes on nowadays, I would think you'd take a lot more precautions. I wouldn't expect any woman living alone to be so lax."

"Maxine, please," Paige's father said, obviously trying to silence her.

But Paige wept harder than before, and Camille hugged her again. Now Paige wished Camille hadn't called her parents at all, because it wasn't like they really wanted to be there. Their mother could be so trifling, self-righteous, and cold sometimes, and Paige wished she would leave.

"Honey, can I get you anything?" Camille asked. "Something to drink maybe?"

"No, I'm fine," she said, and two detectives came over and stood in front of them, one male and one female.

"Miss Donahue, I'm Detective Johnson, and this is my partner, Detective Anderson," the woman said. "We are truly sorry about what just happened to you, but if we could, we'd like to ask you a few questions."

Paige slowly lifted her head again and tried making herself more comfortable on the sofa. "Okay."

Detective Johnson opened a miniature notebook and pulled a pen from her jacket. "Can you tell us what time you went to bed?"

"Maybe around eleven, I think."

The detective jotted down a few words and then asked, "At what time did you realize someone was in your home?"

"Around two o'clock. I was in a deep sleep, but suddenly I heard glass shattering and other loud noises and that's when I glanced at the clock and reached for the phone. But he stormed into my room right away and grabbed it from me."

"Uh-huh," Detective Johnson said. "And what happened next?"

Paige gave them every detail she could think of and hoped this would be all the information they needed.

But Detective Johnson continued. "Do you remember seeing any strangers in your neighborhood earlier yesterday or anytime recently?"

"No. I don't."

"How about a possible description?" Detective Anderson said, chiming in. He seemed like a nice enough man, but she was already becoming a bit tired of all the interrogating. "I realize it was probably pretty dark in your room, but were you able to see his face? Maybe from the moonlight possibly?"

Paige knew she had but calmly said, "No. I couldn't see anything. It all happened so fast, and he was so violent."

"Did he have any weapons?" Detective Johnson asked, writing additional notes.

"Yes, a handgun. And that's what he kept hitting me with," she said, realizing she hadn't mentioned the gun before now. She'd told them how he'd struck her several times but not how.

Detective Anderson looked toward the front doorway. "I see you have an alarm system, so is there some reason it wasn't set?"

Paige saw her mother eyeing her with an I-told-you-so look on her face, but she ignored her.

"I guess I was so upset after Owen left I forgot."

"Owen?" Detective Anderson said.

"My boyfriend. We broke up a few hours before I was raped," she said and then forced more tears from her eyes for credibility. "I don't know how I could have been so careless."

The detectives were called into the kitchen by one of the officers, and all Paige could think was how Owen and she couldn't have ended their relationship at a better time because, without even knowing it, his proposing to her and her not accepting had indirectly given her a solid alibi. She hadn't been all that worried anyway, not with how well the rape had been staged, and also because her close friend Derrick Nelson had agreed to help her out with everything. But still—this *alibi* made her feel a bit more at ease. Although, when it came to Derrick, she couldn't deny that when she'd first told him what she was planning to do, he'd thought she was joking, and then when he'd realized she was dead serious, he'd thought she was insane. But she'd begged him and insisted that she couldn't do this without him. She'd also reminded him of all the times he'd slept around on his wife and how she'd covered for him on too many occasions—how she'd even allowed him to use her condo whenever she was out of town with a client. So it hadn't taken Derrick long to realize how much he owed Paige and that as her friend he was obligated to do what she asked. Plus, it wasn't as if he'd had to have real sex with her. He'd only had to help make things appear that way. What she'd done instead was make sure she and Owen had engaged in very rough sex just a few hours before so the rape kit exam—something she knew the detectives would suggest she have—would prove that sex had actually taken place.

When the detectives returned, Detective Johnson said, "We were just looking at the window inside your back door, but the fingerprints look a bit too small to be a man's. We'll run them anyhow, though, but more than likely they're yours."

Paige nodded but knew they had to be hers and not Derrick's, because he'd worn gloves the whole time.

"So," Detective Anderson said, "did it seem as though the intruder knew exactly where you were? Because if you heard glass crashing in the kitchen but didn't have time to call for help, he must have come straight to your bedroom."

Paige wished Detective Anderson would leave all the questioning to Detective Johnson, because he was starting to unnerve her.

"To be honest, I'm not sure, but he did make it to my room pretty quickly."

"Was the breakup with your boyfriend a bad breakup?" Detective Anderson asked, totally changing the subject. "Was there a lot of arguing or did he threaten you in any way?"

Paige wrinkled her forehead. "No. But you don't think Owen is the person who did this, do you?"

"We have to check all possibilities," Detective Johnson said.

"Well, I can promise you, it wasn't him, because I heard the man's voice. Plus, this guy felt much bigger and was a lot taller than Owen."

Camille, Pierce, and Paige's parents looked on in silence, and finally when the detectives finished questioning her, Detective Johnson said, "I think that's it for now, Miss Donahue. But we definitely want you to have a full examination. That way we can obtain a semen sample."

"That's fine, but the strangest thing about all of this is that this man was actually decent enough to put on a condom. So I'm not sure you'll be able to find anything," she said, knowing they truly *wouldn't* find anything, not even from Owen, since he always wore protection without fail.

"Perpetrators who wear condoms don't do it because they care about their victims or about themselves," Detective Anderson said. "They usually only do it because they don't want to leave behind any DNA. Although if we find stray hairs or skin cells, we'll be able to use that, too."

Paige wasn't sure why she looked at her mother, but as soon as she did, she regretted it. Her mother seemed disgusted and sickened by what had happened, and she could tell her mother thought she deserved whatever she got. It was as if she thought Paige had asked to be raped. Of course, in reality, she *had* asked for it, but her mother didn't know that and had no right blaming her. She had no reason to treat Paige this way, but who was Paige kidding? Maxine Donahue really didn't care one way or the other, because her number one girl was Camille and not much else mattered.

The police officers gathered and documented any evidence they could, and Detective Johnson came back over to Paige. "Can we take you to the hospital now?"

"Is it okay if my sister takes me? I really need her," Paige said, thinking how this would create another opportunity for her to do some serious bonding with Camille, making Camille think she couldn't go through this without her. Although, Paige *was* really concerned about her niece and nephew and said, "Is someone home with PJ and Crystal?"

"I called our next door neighbor right before we left on our way over here, so she's there with them," Camille assured her.

"Good. Well, if you don't mind..."

"Don't say another word," Camille said, standing.

Paige stood, too, and hugged her sister. "Once I come out of the restroom, I'll be ready."

Detective Johnson followed Paige. "Miss Donahue? We'll go ahead and follow you to the hospital, and also, if you can manage, please don't use the restroom or wash any part of your body, because remember, even though your perpetrator used a condom, we still might find DNA from other sources."

"Oh that's right. I think I can hold out a little while longer then. Oh, and Detective, can you have someone come out to cover my backdoor window until morning?" she asked with tears rolling down her face again.

The detective rested her hand on Paige's back. "Of course. No problem."

"Thank you so much. I'll just grab my jacket and purse then," Paige said and then went into her bedroom, turned on the light, and looked into the mirror over her dresser.

She stared at her bruises and sighed with much relief. She was satisfied with a job well done.

Chapter 4

$\mathcal{P}$aige nestled her body further into Pierce's beautiful sleek black Mercedes S550, leaned her head all the way back, closed her eyes, and enjoyed the ride to the hospital. She and Camille were both sitting in the back, and Paige was in pure heaven. She'd been wanting her own Mercedes for some time now, and she was thrilled to know that she was finally only months and possibly only weeks away from having one—this particular Mercedes right here to be exact. She was excited because it was only a matter of time before Pierce removed Camille's name from the title and added hers. It wouldn't be long before she'd be driving it whenever she wanted to, and for the first time in Paige's life, she wouldn't be seen as the underdog. For the first time ever, people would love and respect her and treat her with dignity, and she would be accepted by the "in" crowd. She'd be able to intermingle with high society and well-to-do folks the way she'd always dreamed about, and her parents would never be able to hurt her again. She would receive from Pierce what she'd never gotten from them, and life would finally be good for her.

"Sweetie, are you okay?" Camille asked, and Paige slightly opened her eyes and gazed at her.

Paige sniffled and wiped forced tears. "Yeah, I guess so. But I still can't believe this has happened. I feel so violated."

"I can only imagine, but we're going to be here for you no matter what."

It wasn't quite daylight, but Paige still saw Pierce looking in her direction through his rearview mirror. "We'll be here for as long as you need us."

"I really appreciate that. I appreciate you both."

"And don't you worry," he said. "They'll find this guy eventually."

"I hope so. Because if they don't, I doubt I'll sleep peacefully again."

"Well, in the meantime, you'll come stay with us."

"Absolutely," Pierce agreed.

Bingo. This was the invite Paige had been waiting for and the reason she'd played the woe-is-me bit ever since Camille and Pierce had arrived at her condo. She had to pretend, though, that she didn't want to be a bother to either of them.

"Are you sure? Because I would never want to be an intrusion."

"Of course we are," Camille answered.

"We wouldn't hear of anything different," Pierce added.

Paige did her normal bursting-into-tears routine again and reached over and hugged her sister. "I don't know how I'll ever be able to thank you guys. This is truly very kind of you."

Pierce stopped at the red light and said, "You're family, Paige, and you can stay for as long as you need to."

"You're my sister, girl, and I love you," Camille said. "I always have, and you know I'll do whatever I can to help you."

"I know that, but if you want, I'm sure Karla wouldn't mind my staying with her," Paige said, referring to her best friend.

"Yes, I'm sure she wouldn't, but I'd feel a lot better if you stayed with us so we can protect you. And it's not like we don't have room."

"I'm sure I could also stay with Mom and Dad, too, if it came down to it," Paige said, knowing she would never spend one night with those people and only mentioned them because she wanted Camille to believe she really was trying to find other options and didn't want to invade their lives and privacy. She wanted Camille to think that her coming to live with them was solely Camille's idea and not hers. That way when Paige broke her and Pierce up, no one would be able to say that Paige had weaseled her way into their lives on purpose and then caused the downfall of their marriage. It was true that she was doing all of the above, but no one would ever be able to prove it.

"We even have an extra room with a desk where you can set up a temporary office," Camille went on. "So how can you possibly say no?"

Paige smiled. "I'm so blessed to have you, Camille. I'm blessed to have you both."

"Everything is going to be fine," Camille told her.

Paige leaned against the headrest and closed her eyes again. Her plan was still running smoothly and right on schedule, and now all she had to do was get through this rape kit examination. As she'd told the detectives, she doubted they would find anything, but she figured she'd better do whatever they asked so as to eliminate any unnecessary suspicion.

They drove maybe another ten minutes, and when they pulled into the parking lot of Covington Park Memorial, Paige saw the two detectives parking right next to them. She'd hoped they'd possibly changed their minds about meeting her at the hospital, but since they hadn't, Paige was ready to provide them with another award-winning performance. She would do whatever it took to fool them.

When she opened the car door, Pierce rushed around the vehicle and helped her outside of it. Gosh, was his hand soft and warm, and she wished she could hold on to it forever. What she wouldn't do to hold him tight the way any wife ought to be able to hold her husband—and she could have, if it hadn't been for that doggoned Camille hovering over them and breathing down their necks.

"Thanks so much, Pierce," Paige said.

"Anytime."

Camille wrapped her arm around Paige, and they strolled toward the emergency room entrance. Detectives Johnson and Anderson walked directly behind them.

"We've already called ahead," Detective Johnson said. "So I'll just escort you back to the examination area once we're inside."

"Won't I need to register and give them my insurance card?"

"They'll take care of that as we go along. That way, you won't have to answer any questions in front of others who are standing in line or sitting nearby in the waiting area."

"That's good to hear," she said, walking through the automatic doorway.

"Do you want me to come back there with you?" Camille said, caressing her sister's back.

"Would you?" Paige said with tear-filled eyes.

"Sweetie, of course. I told you, I'm here for you, and I meant that."

Paige swallowed hard and hugged her sister for the umpteenth time, pretending that she loved and appreciated Camille with the utmost sincerity. She did what she had to do—for the time being.

Chapter 5

The examination hadn't been as bad as Paige had thought it would be, and now she sat on the side of the beautiful sleigh bed in one of her sister's guest bedrooms. She was exhausted, sleepy, and feeling out of sorts, but she knew she couldn't put off calling Karla any longer. As it was, she hadn't called her right after the incident, and she knew Karla was going to be livid.

Paige pulled out her BlackBerry and dialed her best friend.

Karla answered right away, but her tone was groggy. "Hello?"

"Hey."

"Paige?"

"Yeah, it's me."

"Is something wrong?" she asked, and Paige could almost see her sitting straight up in bed, now fully awake. Especially since it was only seven a.m., and on Saturdays Karla was never up before nine.

"Actually, there is. I was raped last night."

"You were what? Raped? When? And why are you just calling me?"

"I knew you were going to be upset, but it all happened so fast. Then, once I contacted 911 and called Camille, all I could do was lie across my bed until the police arrived."

"Oh my God, Paige. You really should have called me. And who did this to you?"

Paige told her everything—not the part about her rape being staged or that Derrick had served as her loyal accomplice—but she conveyed everything else she could think of.

"I just don't believe this," Karla said.

"I know. I'm still in shock myself. I can't seem to stop crying, and my nerves are totally shot."

"Okay, look. Let me go, so I can get dressed and be on my way over."

"You don't have to do that. I mean, you can come later if you want, but Camille insisted that I stay with them for a while, so that's where I am."

"Well, I'm glad you're not alone. Although you know you could have moved in with me as well."

Paige wasn't shocked by Karla's offer, and this was the real reason she hadn't been so quick to call her before now. She hadn't wanted to take the chance on Karla extending an invitation before Camille had. "I appreciate that, girl, and if I start to feel like I'm in the way over here, I may take you up on that." Paige knew that would never happen, but she didn't want to sound ungrateful either.

"I hope you will. Although I'm sure you're very comfortable with all the space Camille and Pierce have."

"Yeah, it really is very nice," Paige said, thinking about the fact that this gorgeous home of her sister's would soon be hers.

"So, did the police find any evidence?" Karla asked.

"No, and without any semen or fingerprints, I'm not sure they ever will."

"Criminals always make some sort of mistake. There are certainly a lot of unsolved cases out there, but for the most part, they always get caught."

Paige didn't like the sound of that, but at the same time she wasn't all that worried, because no crime had actually happened. There was the physical battering that Derrick had inflicted upon her, but when it came to the police finding some random rapist, Paige knew they were searching for someone who didn't exist. So again, there was absolutely and positively nothing to be concerned about.

Still, Paige responded by saying, "I really hope they do, Karla. I hope they find this guy and send him away for decades."

"I'm sure they will. And hey, P, is there anything I can do at all?"

"No, just hearing your voice is helping me already, and I'm so sorry I didn't call you sooner."

"I'm sorry, too, but I also understand how upset you must have been and that it was probably a major undertaking just calling for help."

"It was. The whole thing was a living nightmare."

"Gosh," Karla said. "I honestly don't know what to say."

"I know."

"Are you sure you don't want me to come over?"

"Yes. Plus, if I can, I really wanna try to get some sleep."

"Okay, then I'll just drop by this afternoon. I'll call you first, though."

"Sounds good."

"You take care of yourself, girl, and you know I love you."

"I love you, too, Karla."

When Paige ended the call, she removed her velour hooded sweatsuit and slipped on the hot pink silk pajamas Camille had loaned her. Then she lay down, exhaled, and thought about Pierce. He'd been so gentle with her when she'd stepped out of the vehicle at the hospital, and if Camille hadn't rushed to help her when they'd arrived home, she and Pierce could have had more intimate time together. They couldn't make love just yet, but simply being in his presence and having the opportunity to touch him was enough for the time being. She'd wanted this man for years, and it was hard to believe she was finally going to have him. She also couldn't be happier about living under the same roof with him, which would be for a nice little while, since she wasn't planning to move back to her own place until she'd done everything in her power to end his marriage. She wouldn't cause problems for Camille and Pierce right out of the gate, not today or tomorrow, but she also wouldn't let more than a week or two go by before she initiated a massive blowup between them. She would slowly but surely place doubt in Pierce's mind about his loving wife and do the same with Camille about her husband. She'd have them hating each other, and that's when she'd make her move to destroy their union permanently. She would carefully and strategically lure Pierce away from her sister, and he would never want to go back to her. He would wish he'd never married her in the first place and would thank Paige for freeing him from his unhappy situation. It was true that right now he didn't actually know how unhappy he was, but Paige was going to make things crystal clear for him. She'd make him see that Camille wasn't his soul mate after all, nor was she the woman he was destined to live the rest of his life with. He would soon know that *Paige* was the real woman of his dreams and the only woman who could satisfy him completely.

Chapter 6

*I*t was Sunday morning. Paige took a well-needed stretch, opened the pewter-trimmed glass shower door, and stepped through it. She'd turned the water on just before cleansing her face, and now it was hot. It seemed to take a bit longer warming up than her own shower did, but she knew it was because the water had a much lengthier distance to travel in such a huge house.

Paige held her head back, allowing the water to soothe the front of her body, and wished she could stand there forever. It was wonderfully relaxing to her muscles, so she definitely needed this. Yesterday she'd planned on taking a long, hot bubble bath, but as it had turned out, she'd slept well into the afternoon and had only gotten up and gone downstairs when her parents and Karla had come over to see her. Needless to say, things hadn't fared too well with her mother, and it hadn't been ten minutes before Maxine had gotten on her nerves. It was at this point that Paige had begun conversing only with Karla, and had soon heard her mother telling Paige's father they were leaving.

Then once they were gone, Karla and Camille had tried getting Paige to eat something, but she'd pretended she was still too upset to eat anything. Of course, in all honesty, she'd been starving but hadn't let on, because she'd needed Camille to continue feeling sorry for her. She did, however, feel bad about Karla, who'd been devastated and in tears. She'd been terribly hurt over what had happened to Paige, but there was just no way Paige could tell her the truth—that she'd planned the whole incident down to every dirty detail. She would never admit how she'd mapped out, plotted, and schemed her way into Camille and Pierce's private life or how she was only weeks away from winning the grand prize. She couldn't tell her that she'd only done what she had to do so she could finally be happy.

But the worst part of yesterday's activities had been the conversation she'd been forced to have with Owen. She could still hear his distraught tone even now.

"Baby, why didn't you call me? The police were just here, asking me questions about our breakup. Then they told me you'd been raped."

"Because I just couldn't," she'd said. "I couldn't burden you with something like this, not when we're no longer together."

"But baby, you really should have called me. Are you okay?"

"I'm as well as can be expected . . . I guess."

"I am so, so sorry."

"It's not your fault, and I hate those detectives even contacted you. Especially when I told them the guy who raped me was much taller and bigger than you are."

"They were only doing their jobs," he'd said, "and I'm glad they're really trying to find this maniac."

"It was awful," she'd said in a believable, trembling, and very shaky voice.

"I'm sure it was, baby, and I could just kill whoever did this to you."

Paige hadn't said anything else, and once Owen had begged to see her, to no avail, he'd finally told her he would at least call back to check on her later in the evening—although when he had,

Paige had let all three of his calls go to voicemail. She sort of felt bad, since she could tell how concerned he was about her, but it was simply best that Owen move on and forget about her. It was better for him to leave well enough alone and find a woman who truly wanted him.

When Paige finished showering, she stepped out, toweled herself dry, and walked in front of the mirror above the vanity. Her face was still extremely swollen, and she looked horrid. She even had a black eye and hadn't wanted Pierce to see her this way yesterday. Although, as it had turned out, seeing how pitiful she looked had only caused him to empathize with and care about her even more, something she'd noticed when she'd seen him gazing at her. He'd clearly felt sorry for her and probably would have quickly taken her into his arms had his little wifey gone into another room where she belonged. Just thinking about Camille and how she was always in the way made Paige cringe.

Paige saturated her body with a generous amount of shea butter, got dressed in a mustard-colored velour sweatsuit, and went down to the kitchen. When she arrived, she saw Camille setting out her breakfast dishes at the center of the table near the patio doors and Pierce, PJ, and Crystal laughing, talking, and preparing to eat. They all greeted Paige, and Paige hugged both her niece and nephew and took a seat. She'd first considered sitting closer to Pierce, but then decided it was best she sit toward the other end.

"So, did you sleep well last night?" Pierce asked, lowering the sports section of the *Chicago Sun-Times*.

"Not really, but I did get a couple of naps in here and there," she said, knowing she'd slept like a two-day-old baby.

"I know it's hard right now," Camille said, chiming in. "But things will get better as time goes on."

Paige smiled at her sister. "I sure hope so." *Geez. Can't you see*

that Pierce and I were having a nice one-on-one conversation that had
nothing to do with you? So why couldn't you just stay out of it?

The family chatted about this and that, but when Camille took her seat, Pierce said grace.

"Father God, we come right now, thanking You for all You've done, all that You are doing currently, and all that You are surely going to do in the future. We thank You for keeping our family in good health and for allowing my sister-in-law to be here with us. Then, Father, we thank You for the food we are about to receive and for my beautiful wife who prepared it. We humbly ask that You please bless this food, Father, as we use it for the nourishment of our bodies and for our overall strength. With these and many other blessings we ask in your son Jesus' name. Amen."

Paige took a sip of orange juice and then bit into a piece of sausage. "So are you guys going to church this morning?"

"Pierce and the children are," Camille said. "But I'm staying here with you."

"I'll be fine. You'll only be gone a couple of hours, anyway, right?"

"Yeah, but I don't want to leave you all alone."

"I'm telling you, I really will be okay, because all I'm planning to do is head back upstairs to get a little more sleep. Plus, Karla said she was going to stop by around noon."

Camille hesitated but then said, "Well, only if you're sure. Because actually, I am supposed to meet with our women's auxiliary right after service to discuss our upcoming luncheon."

"I told you, sis, I'll be fine. So just go. Enjoy the service and take care of your business."

"If you say so."

"I do."

"Auntie Paige, I can stay here with you, too, if you want," Crystal said.

Paige smiled. "Why thank you, sweetheart, but I'm good. Really I am."

Pierce buttered one of Camille's homemade biscuits and said, "Well, if you need anything, all you have to do is call us. You have both our cell numbers, and of course, if something else comes up, there's always 911."

"And we'll also make sure to leave you the alarm code so you can set it as soon as we leave and then disarm it when Karla gets here," Camille said.

"Will all of you please stop worrying about me?" Paige said, laughing.

"We can't help it, Aunt Paige," PJ told her. "We just don't want anything else happening to you."

"I know that, honey, and you have no idea how much I appreciate that. But for the last time, Montgomery family, I'm going to be fine."

Now they all laughed, and Paige knew they had no idea how fine she truly was going to be just as soon as they backed out of that driveway of theirs and drove down the street. She would be fine because she'd finally have her first chance at accessing the information she needed—information that would prove priceless.

Chapter 7

$\mathcal{T}$he Montgomerys hadn't been gone five full minutes when Paige dashed up to Camille's office. However, now that she'd arrived, she was outraged. Camille didn't even have a real job, yet the entire room screamed style and refinement and was much bigger than the one she had at her condo. The office was filled with expensive cherry-wood furniture that included a fancy desk, matching working table, wall-to-wall bookcases, and a classic black leather sofa. It was enough to make Paige despise her sister even more. Not to mention, while she'd said it many times before, she couldn't help saying it again: Camille had everything, and it just wasn't fair. It wasn't right, and if Paige had things her way, Camille would end up miserable, destitute, and even suicidal. She would practically lose her mind once Pierce filed for a divorce, asked her to move out, and then settled with her for the least amount of alimony possible. Of course, the children would be welcome to live with their father and favorite auntie for as long as they wanted, but if they chose instead to reside with their mother, Paige had no objection to Pierce paying child support. Paige loved her niece and nephew with all her heart, and she would never hurt or deprive them of anything.

Paige sat in front of Camille's computer and clicked on the

AOL icon. She waited for the sign-on screen to open, and as expected, Camille's password was saved in the system and Paige easily accessed her email account. At first she browsed through Camille's inbox listing, without opening any of the messages, and then she opened a new window so she could send out the following email to WilliamT@pmail.com, a fictitious email address Paige had created last week through some off-brand mail server for Camille's fictitious lover, William Tanner:

Dearest William:

I hope this note finds you well, and that you had a great weekend. I haven't been able to call because my sister was raped on Friday evening, and it has really taken a toll on all of us. They haven't caught the guy who did this yet, so she'll be staying here with us for a while. I'll make sure to call you tomorrow, though, right after I drop the children off at school. I can't wait to speak to you again, and I'm getting to the point where I'd really like to see you, William. I know it's wrong to want you so much, but I'm so tired of fighting all these feelings.

Again, I'll phone you in the morning.

With love,
Camille

Paige hit the send icon, printed out a hard copy of the message, deleted it from Camille's sent messages folder, and then signed into William's email account and began typing:

My Dearest Camille:

I'd been hoping I would hear from you today, and please know that I am truly sorry to hear about your sister. Tragedy is never easy on anyone, so I do pray that things get better for her and that they find the person who did this. And as far as you and me, I couldn't be happier about your finally wanting to spend time with me, because you know I've wanted that for months now. Anyway, let's talk more about it when you call tomorrow morning.

So looking forward to hearing your voice.

With all my love,
William

Paige printed out both the email William had received from Camille and also the one he'd just sent back to her. Then she signed back into Camille's account, printed the email from William, and then deleted it from Camille's inbox. This way, she now had both the outgoing copies from each of them as well as both the incoming ones.

Paige signed out of AOL, turned off Camille's computer, and felt proud. She left the office and strolled down the plush-carpeted hallway toward her room, but stopped while passing Camille and Pierce's master suite. In the five years since they'd built their home, she'd gone in there many times, but she wanted to see it again and all by her lonesome.

She pushed the door completely open, walked in, and felt worse than she had when she'd entered Camille's office. The black and off-white color scheme was tremendous, the California king sleigh bed with leather headboard and footboard was adorned with the most striking velvet comforter, matching shams, sheets, and pillowcases, and the matching velvet drapes and off-white Berber carpet were to die for. There was also the stunning marble fireplace situated in the sitting area, right in front of the balcony, as well as the mansion-size walk-in closet Pierce and Camille shared. Paige was in total awe and couldn't believe this was all going to be hers in the near future. She likely wouldn't change a thing except possibly the paint color to a slightly lighter crème than what her sister had chosen. Although as she looked more closely at the carpet, she could see maybe choosing a different texture for her and Pierce's bedroom, and she was sure he'd be fine with making any changes she wanted. He'd always allowed Camille to do whatever made her happy, and she knew he would offer her the same courtesy. He would want the absolute best for his new wife and would do anything to see that she had it.

Just thinking about the fabulous life she'd soon be living gave her tiny goose bumps and made her feel as though she'd finally be special—just as special as Camille had always been to their parents and everyone around them, and maybe even more so. Pierce would treat her like a queen, and she knew they would be happy until death.

Paige went inside the walk-in closet, scanned Camille's section of it, and decided right then that she was going to have every one of these items. Camille must have had every high-end shoe she could think of—Christian Louboutin, Bally, Gucci, Salvatore Ferragamo—and then there were her beautiful handbags: Louis Vuitton, Jimmy Choo, Marc Jacobs, etc., etc., etc. It just didn't make sense, especially since Camille *never* got excited about brand names or any other luxuries she'd been blessed with. As a matter of fact, most of the pricey items she owned had been given to her by Pierce as gifts, because whenever Camille shopped, she looked for serious bargains at normal department stores and only tended to buy things she actually needed or clothing for the children. Paige, on the other hand, was planning to shop for the best of everything, every chance she got, and wouldn't feel bad about it.

About a half hour after Paige had gone back to her own room, the doorbell rang. She smiled, because even though it wasn't quite noon yet, she knew it was Karla. So she went down the winding staircase, disarmed the security system with the code Camille had recited to her, and let her in.

"Hey, honey," Karla said, hugging her.

"Hey yourself, and look at you all dressed up in that tight-fitting black sweater dress."

"Well, we do what we can," Karla said, laughing as they walked into the family room and sat down on the apple red, grained-leather sofa.

"With a dress like that, you'll find a new man in no time. Because I know there had to be a ton of them checking you out this morning."

"Yeah, I guess, but since I went to the early service and wanted to come by here, I sort of hurried out to my car when it was over. And it's not like I'm in a huge hurry to meet anyone anyhow."

"You will be eventually."

Karla's face softened, revealing a touch of sadness. Paige knew why and rubbed the top of her best friend's hand.

"You will," Paige said. "You'll see."

"Maybe, but I won't even lie, P. I miss Kevin so much, and to be honest, I'm not sure any man could ever replace him. That's why I'm not all that interested in meeting someone else so quickly."

Kevin and Karla had only been engaged a month when he'd been killed by a drunk driver, and Paige completely understood how hard it must have still been for her. Especially since it had only happened six months ago.

"I know it's tough," Paige told her. "But as time goes on, you'll feel better and better."

"I sure hope so. But enough about me. How are you?"

"Still hanging in there."

"Have you heard anything from the police? Are there any leads yet?"

"No, nothing at all."

"It's too bad you couldn't see his face."

"I know. I keep thinking the same thing," Paige said, hating all the lying she kept doing to Karla.

"Well, at least it's over," Karla said, scanning the family room and kitchen. "And it's good you have people who love you like Camille and Pierce."

"That's for sure. They've been extremely wonderful to me."

"And you have me, too, remember?"

"Of course, and I won't ever forget that."

"And hey, wait a minute. Where's Owen? Is this his weekend to stay over at the fire station? I just thought about him."

"Girl, long story short, he came over on Friday evening and proposed to me, but I told him I wasn't ready for marriage. And we broke up."

"Oh no. I'm so sorry, P. I had no idea."

"It was all for the best, because I just didn't love him the way he wanted me to."

"Well, as long as you're not upset about it."

"I'm not. I mean, I feel bad for Owen, because I can tell he really loves me, but he'll get over it."

Paige and Karla chatted for another hour, ate some leftover pizza, and then Karla prepared to leave.

"You look tired, so I'm going to let you get some rest."

"Yeah, I am a little sleepy, but I'm so happy you came over. It gives me such peace every time I see you."

"I'm glad. And I'll be back tomorrow, too. I have a meeting after work, so it might not be until early evening."

"That's fine. And if you can't get back until later in the week, then just call me."

"I will," she said as they walked to the front door. "And you take care of yourself, you hear me?"

"I will. I love you, Karla."

"I love you, too."

Paige waved at Karla one last time and watched her drive away. Then she closed the door, went upstairs, and climbed into bed. She tried making herself comfortable, but it wasn't long before her thoughts got the best of her... and she began calculating her next move.

Chapter 8

As soon as Paige and Camille walked inside Paige's condo, Paige shut the alarm off and tossed her shoulder bag onto the purple loveseat. This morning when she'd gotten up, she'd told Camille that she needed to get her laptop, files for her clients, and more clothing. So they'd dropped the children off at school and then driven over. Paige had wanted to laugh during their ride, because it was at that very time that Camille should have been calling her phantom love interest, William. Needless to say, she hadn't known she was supposed to, but it would certainly look like she had on paper when the time was right.

Paige sorted through the junk mail that must have come on Saturday and laid it on an end table. Camille looked on and said, "Maybe you should just have your mail forwarded to our house for a while."

"I guess I could, but for now, I think I'll just leave it as is. Plus, it's not like I'm going to stay with you guys forever."

"There you go again," Camille said, pursing her lips playfully.

"I'm serious. I don't want to overstay my welcome, so as soon as I'm feeling better and like I'm safe, I'm moving back home."

"In due time."

They went into Paige's bedroom, and Camille sighed when

she saw the sheets still tousled across the bed and bloodstains on the pillowcase. Paige hadn't paid attention to any of this on Friday evening, but she knew the blood had likely come from her bleeding lip. It was interesting, though, how Camille seemed much more bothered by all of this than she was, but then Paige knew something Camille didn't, that no actual crime had been committed.

Paige slid open her closet door, pulled out a couple of pairs of jeans, two turtleneck and two V-neck cashmere sweaters, and a sweatsuit, and then pulled out a garment bag. Camille took the items while Paige unzipped her luggage and then passed them back to her. When Paige laid her clothing inside, she went over to her dresser and pulled out underwear and tights, but then she sat down on the bed.

"Come sit with me, sis," Paige said, realizing it was time for a bit of fake bonding.

"Sure. What's up?"

"You know, I never could have gotten through these last couple of days without you, and I won't ever be able to thank you enough."

"Awww. It's nothing at all, and it's like I keep telling you. I love you, and I would do anything for you, Paige."

"I love you, too, and I'm glad you're my big sister."

"I'm glad, too, and actually it's been really nice having you at our house because it reminds me of all the happy times we shared as children."

Paige heard her but couldn't have disagreed more. There was *nothing* happy about her childhood. Still, she nodded and forced a smile onto her face.

"We had so much fun, and Mom and Dad took us on so many amazing summer vacations. Disney World, Disneyland, SeaWorld, Niagara Falls, Hollywood, New York, Miami Beach.

We went somewhere different every single year, and remember how all our friends would be so jealous?"

Paige abruptly left the edge of the bed and placed her underwear inside one of the smaller sections of her bag.

"Are you okay?" Camille asked, sounding confused. "Did I say something wrong?"

Paige wanted to shout a resounding, *Yes, there's a lot wrong!* But she held her tongue and tried moving past her pain and anger. "I'm fine."

"Are you sure?"

"Positive. No, wait. Everything isn't fine when it comes to Mom and Dad or my childhood. They treated me like I was some foster child they didn't want, Camille, and the only reason you didn't notice is because they treated you like royalty."

"What? You really feel that way? Why?"

"Because it's the truth. Maybe you had a great childhood, but I was miserable the entire time. I hated living in that house with them, and the best day of my life was when I moved out of there and got my own place. I could barely afford the rent, but it was ten times better than having to deal with them every day."

Camille seemed dumbfounded, and Paige knew she was shocked, because until now Paige had never openly talked about this to anyone, not even Karla or any of her former boyfriends. She'd kept all her pain to herself, but enough was enough.

"I guess I don't know what to say, but I'm so sorry you felt that unhappy."

"It's not your fault," Paige said, knowing she blamed Camille for her misery just as much as she blamed her parents, because it was Camille who they'd highly favored. It was Camille whom they'd given everything to at all costs and then acted as though they didn't have another child.

"Gosh, Paige, I'm stunned."

"I'm sure you are, but like I said, it's not your fault, so just forget it."

"Why haven't you mentioned this to me before now?" Camille wanted to know.

"I just didn't."

"Well, I wish you would have, because regardless of how you think Mom and Dad felt about you back then, I always loved you."

"Maybe."

"Paige, please. You know I did."

"I'm not saying you didn't, but what I do know is that Mom and Dad have never loved me. They tolerated me because they had to. Haven't you ever noticed how distant my relationship has been with them as an adult?"

"I just thought you and Mom had issues because you're so much alike. And then, as far as Dad, he's been a quiet man all his life and never says much to anyone. He's a good person, though."

"Yeah, he is, but he goes along with whatever Mom says or does, and when she treated me badly, all he did was stand by and watch. He never defended me or tried to console me when he knew I was down about it."

"Maybe we need to have a family meeting with just the four of us," Camille suggested.

"Nope. Not interested," Paige said matter-of-factly.

"Sis, sometimes letting everything out is the only way to fix things."

"I'm not having any meeting with them, Camille, and that's that."

"Okay, then, what about seeing a family therapist? That way, you could discuss your childhood, what happened to you on Friday night, and anything else."

"I'm not doing that either. I don't need it."

Thankfully, Camille didn't force the issue, because Paige had no intention of seeing some overrated, overpaid, know-nothing shrink when there wasn't a thing wrong with her. There was no reason to get any counseling when all her problems were about to be solved through Pierce.

After a few minutes, they gathered the rest of Paige's things and went into the living room. They hadn't said much else to each other, so Paige finally spoke.

"I think I'll drive my car back to your house."

"Why? Because I don't mind taking you anywhere you wanna go."

"I'd rather just have my own transportation," she said, and Camille didn't argue.

Finally they loaded the bags they were carrying into each of their trunks and drove away from the condo, Paige in the silver Lexus she couldn't afford and Camille in her shiny black Cadillac Escalade. Camille was a wealthy housewife and carpool mom to her heart, but little did she know, those wealthy little housewife days were coming to an end—so fast she wouldn't know what hit her.

Chapter 9

As soon as Paige hung her clothing in the closet and placed her folded items in the dresser drawer, she went into the extra room where Camille told her she could work, set up her files, and turned on her laptop. Last week, she'd been following up with various media producers for a motivational speaker she represented, and now she was on the phone with Nancy, who worked at a Boston TV affiliate.

"Hey Nancy, it's Paige Donahue, here. How are you?"

"I'm good, Paige. And you?"

"I'm well."

"Did you have a great weekend?"

"I sure did," Paige said as if nothing out of the ordinary had happened in her life. "You?"

"Yeah, it was great. Spent time with the family, and of course, that's always fun."

"I'm glad."

"So, what can I do for you?"

"Well, I just wanted to check in to see if you received the cover letter and press release I emailed you a couple of weeks ago. It was for one of my clients who'll be in town next month speaking at a scholarship dinner."

"As a matter of fact, I did, and was going to be calling you just as soon as I figured out which morning segment we could get him on. Do you know if he's planning to fly in the night before?"

"I'm not sure, but if you need him to, it won't be a problem."

"Why don't we plan on him doing that, so I can get him scheduled around six or six-thirty a.m. This will likely be the best time for his audience, since folks are usually watching and getting ready for work at the same time."

"Sounds good. And you'll email me confirmation?"

"Yes. No later than tomorrow."

"I really appreciate this, Nancy."

"His book sounds very interesting, and one of my colleagues says he's a mesmerizing and very informative speaker. So I'm glad to do it."

"He's definitely very talented, and thanks again."

"Take care now."

This was the kind of thing that made Paige proud, booking a client on a live local network show on the same day as an appearance. It was a great feeling, and she hoped the same thing would happen once she followed up with an FM radio station in New York and the *Atlanta Journal-Constitution* in Atlanta for two other clients. It also looked like the former NFL player she represented was going to be featured in *USA Today* because of his philanthropy efforts, and she couldn't wait to lock that in as well.

When Paige heard a knock at her door, she looked up and said, "Come in." It was Camille, and Paige smiled when she saw her entering with a wooden tray filled with tuna sandwiches, kettle potato chips, and iced tea. Even if Paige wanted to, there was no denying how sweet this was of her sister.

"Wow. Now, you know you didn't have to do this, right?"

"Of course I did. Anything for my baby sister, and especially after all you've been through...lately and in the past."

Camille set the tray down on the chaise, then sat on it herself, and Paige rolled toward her in the desk chair she was sitting in.

"Thank you so much, Camille."

"I figured you might be hungry, and I hope you're able to work okay in here. If not, you can always use my office, which has a full desktop computer, two desks, and lots of shelving."

Paige took a bite of her sandwich. "No, this is perfect."

Camille opened her bag of chips. "Did you call Detective Johnson yet?"

"I did. I called her before I started working, and unfortunately, they still don't have any leads. They did have Owen supply a DNA sample, which matched a hair they found in my bed, and they also found what they believe are the rapist's skin cells from under my fingernails, but there was no match with anyone in their system."

"That's too bad."

"I know. And I'm starting to think they'll never find this person."

"Well, I'm not giving up hope, and I'm going to keep praying they do."

Paige expressed much worry and frustration for Camille's purposes but knew the police would never figure out the truth.

They both ate and drank their tea until Camille folded her arms, her spirit now solemn. "Hey, can I talk to you about something?" she asked.

Paige wasn't sure what this was about and hoped Camille hadn't somehow discovered she'd been snooping around in her office yesterday or that her computer had been used. But then, that couldn't be it, because she wouldn't have fixed such a nice lunch for the two of them.

"Of course. What's up?" Paige said.

"To tell you the truth, I'm not even sure where to begin or why I'm even telling you this."

Paige gave Camille her undivided attention. "This sounds serious."

"Actually, it is. Sort of."

"You're not sick, are you?"

"No, it's nothing like that."

"Then what's wrong?"

"It's Pierce and me."

"What about you?"

Camille took a deep breath. "For the first time, I feel like we're slowly drifting apart."

Paige was flabbergasted but also wanted to jump for joy. She'd had no idea her sister and Pierce were having problems. Not when they seemed so happy with each other.

"Why do you think that?" Paige asked, desperately wanting to know.

"Because we are. When you've been happily married for fifteen years and then suddenly something feels different, you just know."

"How long have you felt like this?"

"For about six months now. I mean, it's not like we don't get along, but we seem to be going our separate ways a lot more than normal. Although it's not like it can really be helped, because over the last year I've really stepped up my involvement with church activities and the children's school events. Plus, I also now volunteer with a domestic violence and women's shelter organization."

"Well, what's wrong with that? Especially since it was only a year ago when you were feeling bored and like you wanted to do a lot more than just cooking, cleaning, and taking the kids to school."

"Yeah, but Pierce doesn't like the fact that I'm not home as much. He feels like I'm now putting my outside activities before our marriage, which isn't true. And then a month ago, he actually suggested that maybe I was tired of him and either wanted or already had someone new."

Paige wasn't sure how to respond to that comment exactly, but what she did know was that this whole trouble-in-paradise scenario was a real blessing. A blessing indeed. For her, anyway, and she couldn't be more elated.

"I just hate this, Paige. I hate what's happening to us after all these years, so maybe it would be best if I gave up all these other things and just went back to being a housewife."

"Is that what you want?"

"No."

"Then I wouldn't give up anything. I mean, you know I love my brother-in-law, but if he really cares about you and respects you, then he'll support whatever it is that makes you happy. He'll stand behind you and will understand that cooking his meals and taking care of the children isn't enough for you."

"Yeah, but I have to admit that, lately, there have been times when I've done so much in a single day that I'm too tired to even make love to him. And that, of course, isn't going over very well."

Good, was all Paige could think, because she didn't want them being intimate on a regular basis anymore.

"Hey, you know what?" Camille said. "Forget I even brought this up."

Paige frowned. "Why?"

"Because my problems are nothing compared to what you've just gone through, and now I'm sorry I even burdened you with them."

"Are you kidding? Camille, I love you, and you can always tell me anything. I mean, come on now, what are sisters for?" she said, standing up and hugging her.

"Thank you, girl. And thank you for listening."

"Anytime. And you just hang in there."

"I'm sure everything will be fine, because one thing I know is that I love Pierce with all my heart, and I know without a doubt that he feels the same way about me."

Paige smiled. "Well, then there's nothing at all for you to worry about, right?"

"Right. Now, you get back to work, missy."

"Yes, ma'am!"

They both chuckled, and Camille left the room. But then she stuck her head back inside the doorway. "Oh, and just so you know, I'm going to head out in about an hour for a school fundraiser meeting, so will you be okay?"

"I'm good. Do you need me to pick up the kids or anything?"

"No, PJ has a soccer game right after school, Crystal is staying after to watch it, and Pierce and I are going as well. Then, when it's over, I have a board meeting. Oh, and do you want me to drop some dinner off to you before then?"

"No, I'll get something on my own."

"Okay, but if you change your mind, just call me."

When Camille left again, Paige wanted to turn flips. She couldn't have been happier about Camille and Pierce's marital woes, and this meant her job of breaking them up was going to be a lot easier than she'd thought. It wouldn't be simple, but she certainly wouldn't have to work as hard as she'd imagined.

Chapter 10

Camille hadn't even been gone a full two minutes and already Paige was perched in front of her sister's computer. The same as yesterday, she signed into Camille's email account and sent William a message:

Dearest William:

It was really great talking to you this morning, and I wanted to let you know that I've made my decision. I'll meet you at the hotel we spoke about at 11. I won't deny that I'm a little nervous, but what's important is that you and I have made such an amazing connection. I realize it's only been through emailing and phone conversation, but I feel as if you are my soul mate. It's also hard to believe that we've never even met and only ran across each other more than a year ago by accident. But I guess that's social networking for you, huh? Anyway, I'll see you tomorrow.

With love,
Camille

Paige sent the email and signed into William's email. She typed a quick response from him to Camille that basically said he was excited to finally meet her and that she wouldn't regret it. Paige hit send and repeated what she'd done yesterday by printing out both the incoming and outgoing messages for the two of them. Then she deleted both from Camille's account again.

She turned off Camille's computer, but when her phone rang, she was glad she'd brought it with her into Camille's office. However, when she picked it up and saw that it was Owen, she scowled and considered letting it go to voicemail.

Still, she went ahead and answered. "Hello?"

"Why haven't you been answering your phone?" he said in a panic.

"I just haven't."

"I've been calling you for two days, and I've been worried sick. If I hadn't gotten you today, I was driving over to your sister's house."

"I'm sorry," she said. "But the truth is, I've been feeling so down and depressed, I haven't felt like talking to anyone."

"Well, I still wish you had at least let me know how you were doing."

"I know, and I apologize."

There was a moment of silence and then Owen said, "You know I still love you, right? I love you, and I miss you terribly."

Paige knew it was best not to say anything, so she didn't.

"Did you hear me?"

"Owen, please let's not do this, okay?"

"Baby, I really thought we had something special, and not being with you really hurts."

Paige hated whiners and rolled her eyes toward the ceiling. "Well, it's like I've been saying, Owen, I'm really sorry about that and I wish things could have turned out differently."

"Then why don't we start over?"

"That won't be possible."

"Why?"

"Because I don't love you," she said bluntly.

"Wow, even after all you've been through, you're still the same ol' selfish Paige."

"No, I'm just being honest."

"You know, it's never good when people play with your emotions and then they just walk away like you never even mattered to them. People should be very careful when they do things like that."

His tone had changed, and Paige wasn't sure how to take it. "I don't know how many times you want me to say I'm sorry, Owen, but I really am."

"You should be," he said and hung up.

Paige set her phone down and didn't know what to think of Owen or his phone call. He'd sounded normal in the beginning, but it was almost as if he'd switched his entire tune toward the end of their conversation and had found the nerve to hang up on her. Jerk.

She picked her phone back up to call one of her clients, but as soon as she did it rang again. This time it was her mother, and Paige groaned. "Hello?"

"So are you feeling better?"

That was just like her mother to jump straight to the point with no greeting, no anything. "I am."

"What are the police saying?"

"Nothing. They have no DNA matches and no suspects."

"Camille told me you checked in with them this afternoon."

"Then why are you asking *me* about it?"

"Because for all I know you could have heard something different just a few minutes ago."

"Whatever, Mom."

"So how long are you plannin' on staying at your sister's? Because I would hate to see you cause problems for her."

"Mom, what in the world are you talking about? Did Camille say something to you?"

"No, Camille, God bless her soul, is very naïve when it comes to you. But I know who you are, Paige. You're a bad seed, and that's why I've never been able to love you the way a mother should."

Paige paused for a few seconds, tears streaming down her face. "Mom, how could you say that to me? How could you say something so cruel?"

"Because it's the truth, and I'll feel a lot better once you've moved back home. Camille has a wonderful husband and two beautiful children, and the last thing they need is you hanging around there."

Tears flooded Paige's face. "Mom, I was raped," she shouted. "Remember? I was raped and beaten with a gun, and you have the nerve to talk to me this way?"

"Well, if you were, then I'm really sorry about that."

"What do you mean, *if*?"

"Well, it just seems awfully strange that this so-called rapist was nice enough to use a condom, and of all nights, you forgot to turn on your security system."

"Are you saying I'm lying?"

"No. Just pointing out facts. Not to mention, I would hope that not even someone as low as you would fake something so serious."

"You know what, Mom? Go to hell."

"No, *you* go to hell! As a matter of fact, you can go anywhere you want as long as you get the hell out of my daughter's house."

Paige was crushed. "But Mom...I'm your daughter, too."

"Biologically maybe, but that's where our relationship ends."

"What?" Paige asked, her heart beating frantically.

"Look," her mother said. "All I want is for you to pack your things and leave Camille's house. You hear me?"

Paige pressed the end button on her phone and threw it onto the desk. She couldn't remember when she'd been so upset. Her mother made her sick, but what worried her was that if Maxine truly believed she was up to something and was going to cause trouble for Camille and Pierce, it wouldn't be long before she mentioned it to them. For all Paige knew, she'd already hinted around to her favorite daughter as a warning. But that wasn't her mother's style, though, and had she already spoken to Camille, her words would have been straight, no chaser, and Camille would have quickly asked Paige about it. Still, Paige couldn't take any chances on her mother messing things up and had to act faster than planned. Instead of a month or so, she would have to drop a major bomb within the next two weeks.

Paige looked back at Camille's computer screen and casually browsed through some of the "real" incoming messages Camille had already opened. She could tell they'd already been read, because they were no longer displaying in bold print. The latest email was from Nordstrom, so Paige opened it to see what Miss Thing had purchased for PJ or Crystal, because she doubted she'd purchased anything for herself. But as she scrolled through the order confirmation, she saw an order for three cashmere sweaters, one in black, one in hot pink, and one in mustard. Then she saw a notation that said, "Ship to: Paige Donahue," and realized Camille was sending her a gift. For a moment, Paige felt a bit guilty, especially since she loved cashmere anything, but it was only for a moment, because seconds later she closed the email, clicked the "Keep As New" button, signed off Camille's computer, and never looked back. Her sister's gesture was kind, but it wasn't enough to make up for all the years her parents had worshiped their little darling yet treated Paige like some orphan. It wasn't enough to stop Paige from getting what she wanted. It wouldn't stop her from taking Pierce.

Chapter 11

The day had sort of flown by, and it had only been seconds ago that Paige had heard Pierce and the children entering the house. So she did a once-over in the mirror, making sure her shoulder-length ponytail was smooth and had no stray hairs flying out of place. Then she slipped on a pair of brand-spanking-new black skinny jeans and a cropped orange sweater. She'd known there would come a time when Camille wouldn't be home and she'd have her first opportunity to flaunt what she had, and it was the reason she'd remembered to pack these two clothing items in particular. She'd done so just this morning when Camille had taken her to her condo. Then, when Camille had told her the great news, that she had a board meeting this evening, Paige had known it was high time for Pierce to see what he was missing. Of course, her face still didn't look its best, but Pierce knew the reason for that and certainly hadn't forgotten what the real Paige Donahue looked like.

Paige waltzed down the stairway and strolled into the kitchen.

"Hey Auntie Paige," Crystal said, smiling brightly and hugging her.

"Hey, sweetie. How was school today?"

"Good. And guess what?"

"What?"

"All the girls in fifth grade are sporting dresses tomorrow, so I have to pick out something really, really cool to wear."

"That sounds like so much fun. I remember when I was growing up, I loved when some of my friends picked out certain days to get all dolled up."

"I know, and I'm so excited," Crystal said.

Pierce laughed at his daughter and shook his head. "How's it goin', Paige?"

"I'm fine. How are you?"

"Tired."

"I'm sure."

"I can't wait for Mom to get home so she can help me pick something out," Crystal interrupted.

"Well, if you want, I can help you start looking, too," Paige told her.

"Would you really?"

"Of course."

"Wow, that would be great, Auntie Paige."

"Girls!" PJ griped, clearly unimpressed. Then he hugged his aunt. "Hey, Aunt Paige."

"Hey honey. So, how was your game?"

"It was great. We won, and we have a super talented team again this year."

"And PJ made half of all the points," Pierce said, beaming.

"Really?" Paige said. "Oh my goodness, PJ, I'm really proud of you."

"Thanks," he said, smiling.

"And once my face heals up a little more, I'll have to come see you play."

"That would be the bomb," he said.

Pierce took a seat at the island and sorted through the mail lying on the granite tabletop. "So, have you eaten, Paige? The kids and I stopped at their favorite restaurant, Fuddruckers, and had ostrich burgers."

"Actually, I have. I ordered some Italian food a couple of hours ago and had it delivered."

"Good," Pierce said and then looked at his children. "So, who has homework?"

"We both do, Dad," PJ said. "And when don't we?"

"Well, it's not like we're paying all that tuition for nothing, right?"

"I guess, but Crissy and I have homework every single night *and* every single weekend. And *she's* only in the fifth grade."

"But that's why you guys have excelled so much educationally. And when you're older, you'll be glad you went to such an esteemed K–12."

"I guess," PJ said.

"You'll see."

"So, you'll be up in a few minutes, Auntie Paige?" Crystal confirmed while grabbing her book bag from the chair.

"Yep."

"See you, Aunt Paige," PJ said, and they both went up to their rooms.

Paige glanced at Pierce and could barely contain herself. She was finally alone with him and was having a hard time trying not to stare at him. He always looked handsome, but for some reason he looked even better to her now, and being this close to him drove her wild. So, as a distraction, she strutted over to the stainless steel double-door refrigerator and pulled out a bottle of Fiji water. She opened it, took a quick drink, and then sat across from Pierce, watching him read what looked to be some banking magazine.

"So," she began. "Camille had another meeting tonight, I guess."

Pierce didn't look up but said, "Yeah, and lately that's pretty much the norm."

"Why do you say that?"

"She's involved with a lot of organizations, and she has a lot of meetings to attend these days."

Paige waited about fifteen seconds and then responded. "Well, actually, I'm going to be honest with you. I mean, I know I shouldn't be saying this, but Pierce, I'm really worried about you and Camille."

"Worried why?"

Paige drank more of her water. "Can we keep this entire conversation between just the two of us? Because Camille would kill me if she knew I was saying anything to you."

"I guess it depends on what it is you have to tell me, because Camille and I have never been in the habit of keeping secrets."

"Then maybe I shouldn't say anything."

"Must not be that important, then," Pierce said, smiling.

"I think it is, but like I said, if Camille knew I was discussing her marital business behind her back, she wouldn't be too happy about it."

"Okay, just this one time, I won't repeat what you say. So, what is it?"

"You promise?"

"You have my word."

"Well, just this afternoon, she was telling me that things haven't been the greatest between the two of you lately, and that you don't like all the time she's been spending away from home."

"That's an understatement."

"So, it's true then."

"Very. She's gone all the time, and we hardly get to spend any time alone together."

"I really hate hearing that, Pierce. And just so you know, my advice to her was that she give up all those church activities, school meetings, and that nonprofit she's been working so closely with."

"You told her that?" Pierce said, sounding surprised.

"I did. I told her that I loved her and that the last thing I wanted was to see her marriage fall apart. I told her how wonderful of a man you were and that nothing was more important than that."

Pierce smiled. "Wow. I really appreciate that, Paige, and it was very kind of you to speak up for me. Especially since you and Camille have always been so close."

"I know, but it wasn't a problem at all."

"So, did she agree with you?"

"She didn't really say one way or the other, but I do believe my words gave her something to think about."

"Well, at least that's a start."

"It is, and I know Camille will do the right thing."

"I hope so, because I really do love and need my wife."

"I hear you, and of course, I'm behind you and Camille a hundred percent."

"You're a good sister-in-law, Paige."

"Don't mention it."

Paige drank the last of her water, got up, and tossed the bottle into a small recycling bin.

"So, there's still nothing much from the police, I hear," Pierce said.

"Nope, not a thing."

"That really bothers me."

"Me too, but what can we do?"

"I guess you're right. I'm sure the police are doing everything they can, and I'm just glad you're doing so well. You seem to be recovering very nicely."

"I am. I'm getting stronger every day...Oh well, I'm going to go see if I can help Crystal and then maybe get a little more work done."

"Okay, and just let the kids or me know if you need anything."

How about you come up to my room so I can show you exactly what it is I need.

"No, I think I'm good," she said. "But thanks, Pierce."

Paige walked away, but her body was on fire. She wanted Pierce right then and there and knew she had to move on to the next phase of things. Her mother had already convinced her of that a few hours ago, what with all her suspicions and accusations, and Paige knew it was time she took care of business. She would do it now or never—and *never* simply wasn't an option.

Chapter 12

*O*ver the last couple of weeks, Paige's swelling had gone down considerably and was basically undetectable, thanks to her mad skills with makeup. Even the black circle under her eye was no longer visible, and she felt a whole lot better. Although her great mood likely had more to do with all that she'd been up to—she'd been a very bad girl over the last few days—and less to do with her physical healing process. She'd finally done her job, and at this point, all she had to do was sit back and enjoy the fireworks—fireworks that were starting now. As expected, Pierce had just stormed up the stairs, yelling out Camille's name, and now he was inside the bedroom screaming at her. Paige opened the door to the guest room so she wouldn't miss a word.

"So, who is this bastard, William, you've been sleeping with?" Pierce shouted.

"William? What are you talking about?" Camille asked.

"You know exactly what I'm talking about. The man you've been seeing and emailing almost every single day over the last two weeks."

"Excuse me?" Camille said, and Paige could only imagine the horrified and confused look on her sister's face. Namely, because Camille really *didn't* have a clue what he was talking about.

"Camille, please don't play stupid with me. Don't insult my intelligence. Not when I have copies of everything."

There was a pause, and Paige guessed Camille was reading through all the email she had anonymously mailed to Pierce yesterday at his work address by overnight service through the U.S. Postal Service. Paige had been very busy over the last week and a half, creating more and more email exchanges between Camille and *William*, and it was finally paying off. She'd also done something different with a number of them, because it had finally dawned on her that if Camille ever looked closely at these messages, she might figure out that they'd all been sent at times when Paige was alone in their house. So what she'd done was schedule five of the latest messages to go out on days and times when she and Camille were together—that day last week when they'd spent the entire afternoon at a spa, last Wednesday and Friday when they'd gone to lunch, and while Camille didn't know it yet, two more would be going out from her to William two days from now on Thursday morning, times when Paige would either be out on business all day or would have moved back home, and William would be responding to each of them. Paige had known about this particular Internet feature for a while and knew she was taking a huge chance that Camille might come straight home from each of the places they'd gone last week and sign into her email. But just as Paige had thought and hoped, Camille hadn't. So once everyone had gone to bed on each of those nights, Paige had tiptoed into Camille's office, printed copies, and deleted all evidence.

"I've never seen these messages a day in my life," Paige heard Camille trying to explain, and Paige hoped her deep thoughts hadn't caused her to miss anything.

Pierce laughed out loud. "My God, Camille, what do you take me for? A complete fool?"

"No, but I really don't know who sent these."

"Do you see your email address on all of them? Those that you sent out as well as those you received back? Do you?"

"No...I mean, yes. I mean, I see them, but what I'm saying is that I didn't send them. I don't even know anyone named William."

"You are such a liar, Camille. You're a lying whore."

"What? Why are you calling me that? And why are you doing this?"

"Because the proof is right here, Camille. It's staring us straight in our faces. And you even had the audacity to tell him how no man, not even I, had ever made you feel the way he does. Then there was another note where you basically bragged about the fact that I thought you were at a church meeting when you were really laid up with him at a hotel."

"But none of this is true, baby. I swear. I swear on our children's lives."

"You're a real piece of work, you know that? I mean, I can't believe you would actually sit here, swearing on PJ's and Crystal's life, knowing good and well you're guilty. Unbelievable."

"But I didn't do anything. I would never, ever sleep around on you, Pierce, and you know that. I would never even talk to another man on the phone. Not unless it was family- or business-related."

"Oh yeah? Then why do a number of the messages say you *have* been calling him?"

"I don't know, but it's not true. You can even check my phone if you want."

Pierce laughed again, his tone markedly cynical. "Oh, like you don't know how to delete phone calls, I guess."

"I'm telling you, this is all a big mistake. These are all lies."

"Well, if that's true, then where did these messages come from?

And how did someone so miraculously send them back and forth from your email address?"

"I don't know. It must be some sort of mistake."

"Okay, let's just say it is. I know it isn't, but just for the sake of conversation. If it's a mistake, why would someone randomly choose you and your email address and then purposely send them to me at the bank?"

"I don't know."

"I mean, who hates you so much that they would try to harm you like this?"

"I don't know. But what I'm telling you is that none of this is true. These are all lies, and I have no idea why this is hap—"

"You know what?" he said, interrupting her. "Just save it, Camille. Save it for someone who's crazy and naïve enough to believe you. I knew when you started spending all that time away from home there was someone else, but I just didn't want to accept it."

"Pierce, please. Baby, you have to believe me," Camille begged in tears, and Paige stood near her doorway smirking and loving every bit of it.

"You make me sick," he said. However, Paige was surprised to hear tears in his voice also. "After all the years we've been together, Camille. After all the years I've gone out of my way to prove how much I love you. And that still wasn't enough for you?"

"Of course it was. And you know how much I love you, too, baby. I've always loved you, and I would never hurt you. I would never sleep with another man. I just wouldn't do something that horrible."

There was silence, and then Paige heard footsteps plodding down the hallway. Next, she heard someone walking down the staircase, and she could tell it was Pierce. Camille rushed behind him, crying hysterically and trying to reason with him, but it wasn't doing any good. Seconds later, a door slammed, and Paige knew Pierce was gone. She wasn't sure if he was gone for good or only for a little while to gather his thoughts, but he was gone just the same and Paige saw that as a plus. It was a sure sign her hard work was paying off nicely and that it wouldn't be long before Pierce came running to her for comfort. It was only a matter of time before her brother-in-law would be hers. Permanently.

Chapter 13

*P*aige waited silently in her room, trying to figure out how she was going to approach Camille, but she knew she had to handle her with kid gloves. She had to console her, make her see that she believed she was innocent, even if Pierce didn't, and that she would stand by her until the end. Paige lingered in her room a few more minutes and then walked out to the top of the staircase. She heard Camille bawling loudly and knew it was time she went to her. When she made it to the main floor, she watched Camille pacing back and forth, wiping colossal tears from her eyes and stroking her hair from front to back. She was a nervous wreck, and Paige pulled her sister into her arms. Camille hugged her back and wailed even louder.

"I'm...so...sorry...you...had...to...witness...that...fiasco... between...Pierce and me," she said between deep breaths and sniffles.

Paige caressed her back with both hands. "Honey, please don't do this. You have to stop crying, okay?"

Camille sobbed even more, but finally after a half hour she quieted down and was able to speak.

"I just don't understand what's going on, because I have no idea what Pierce is talking about. I've never emailed anyone by the name of William in my whole life."

"Of course you haven't, and even if Pierce doesn't believe you, you know I do."

Camille took a couple of steps back and grabbed her sister's hands. "Thank you so much for that, Paige. Thank you for believing in me. And I'm so glad you're here, because I really need you right now."

"I'm glad I'm here, too, and I'll be here for as long as you want."

"You know what?" Camille said, suddenly leaving Paige standing where she was. "I haven't even checked my computer, because when I glanced through all those email messages, they really did have my email address on them."

Paige followed her up the stairs and into her office. Camille sat down and signed into her AOL account. She immediately searched through all of her new mail, old mail, and sent mail, but didn't see anything out of the ordinary or anything with the name William on it. She even checked her folder of deleted messages, and still there was nothing—although Paige could have told her that there wouldn't be. Not when she'd carefully removed all traces of her masterful scheme.

"I just don't get it," Camille yelled. "I don't understand how this could have happened."

"Sweetie," Paige said, standing behind her sister and rubbing her shoulders. "Please try to calm down. There has to be some sort of an explanation for all this, and the truth will prevail. It always does."

"I have to call Pierce," she said, reaching over and lifting the cordless phone from its base and dialing his cell number. Paige had a feeling he wasn't going to answer and knew Camille was wasting her time. But she stood there supporting her efforts in silence. When his voicemail answered, however, Camille left him a message. "Baby, this is Camille. Where are you? I'm so sorry about all of this, but as God is my witness, I don't know any William, and I never sent anyone those emails. Please call me, and please come home. Baby, I'm freaking out here, and I don't want to lose you. I love you so much, so please, please come home, Pierce."

Camille pressed the end button. "Mom and Dad should be bringing the children home pretty soon. They took them out to dinner, and I'm so glad they weren't here a little while ago."

"I'm glad they weren't either. But what are you going to say to them if Pierce doesn't come back tonight?"

"He'll be back."

Paige wasn't so sure about that, and to be honest, she was hoping he wouldn't. She was praying he'd checked in to a hotel and would only return tomorrow for the rest of his things. If she was lucky, he'd already decided to move out for good.

"Maybe I should have given up all of my outside activities. Remember, I was just telling you about all that a couple of weeks ago."

"I know, but why should you have to give up doing things you love? Things that give you fulfillment. You're well-educated, outgoing, and you should be able to do whatever you want."

"Maybe. But my husband should have come first. I should have been a lot more mindful of that."

"I agree with you, but only to a certain extent."

"And why is that?"

"Because every husband should want his wife to be happy. He should want her to be just as happy as he is. Both inside of their home and outside of it."

"Still. If I could do things over, I wouldn't get involved in nearly as many activities or attend so many meetings. And I'm going to do everything I can to make things up to him. I can't and won't lose my husband over something this silly."

Paige knew it was time she raised the bar and placed a bit of doubt and suspicion in her sister's mind, too. "Yeah, but if you think about it, Camille, Pierce never should have accused you of messing around just because you weren't at home the way he wanted you to be. It's almost like he became paranoid for no reason. And as much as I hate saying this, when people accuse you for no reason, it's normally because they're the ones who are guilty of something."

Camille looked at Paige, her forehead wrinkled. "You don't really think that, do you?"

"I'm just sayin'. Because it's not like he's ever accused you of having an affair before now, has he?"

"No."

"Then why would he all of a sudden start accusing you last month, and now he's gone as far as thinking he has proof of it. For all we know, he could have been the one who sent those email messages."

"But why would he do that?"

"I don't know. Maybe so he could justify messing around himself."

Camille stood up, clearly defensive. "I don't think so, Paige, and I wish you wouldn't say things like that about my husband."

Paige hurried to soften her accusation. "Camille, I didn't mean any disrespect, and you know I love Pierce. But at the same time, you're my sister, and I'm always going to look out for you more than I will for him."

"I know, and I appreciate that. But Pierce would never play games like this. He would never have sent those emails."

"I'm sorry," Paige said quickly. "I guess my imagination sort of got the best of me, and I never should have said those things. Please forgive me."

"It's fine," Camille said, walking out of her office. "It's been an upsetting evening for both of us."

"If you want, I can go downstairs and wait for PJ and Crystal to get home, and you can go lie down."

"You don't mind?"

"No, not at all."

"If Mom and Dad come in, just tell them I wasn't feeling well and I'll call them tomorrow."

"I will. And Camille, I really am sorry. There's no doubt that Pierce loves you, and you love him. And when he gets back, the two of you will be able to sit down and figure this all out."

Camille exhaled deeply. "I sure hope so."

Yeah right. You can hope all you want, but sweetheart, your marriage is over.

Chapter 14

It was a chilly yet bright and sunny day in October, and Paige simply couldn't be happier. It was true that Pierce had eventually come home shortly after midnight, but the good news was that he'd slept in the other guest bedroom, and as far as she knew, he hadn't said a word to Camille. Not even this morning when he'd gotten dressed and spent a little time chatting with the children or right before he'd driven off to work. He was still outraged, and Paige couldn't have felt more satisfied or tickled. Things were certainly going her way, and later today she would call her brother-in-law to see how he was doing. She'd make sure he knew she'd always be there for him, the same as he'd been there for her over the last two weeks.

Paige contacted a couple of her clients and then called her good friend Derrick at his office. Derrick owned a private insurance agency, and since he was his own boss, he could talk anytime he wanted.

"Nelson Insurance Agency," the woman said.

"Hey, Ava. It's Paige. How are you?"

"I'm well. And you?"

"I'm good. Is he in?"

"Sure. Hold on a minute."

"Hey stranger," he said after picking up the call.

"Hey yourself, and how are you?"

"With the exception of the few scratches you left on my chest—which thankfully Andrea can't see because of all the hair I have—I'm fine. But it's you I've been pretty worried about."

"I'm doing wonderfully, my friend, and remember we agreed we wouldn't contact each other for a while. You know, so things would have a chance to settle down."

"Well, have they?"

"Pretty much. They found your DNA, but they have no idea who it belongs to. Oh, and for the record," she said, chuckling, "had you not worn a V-neck, there wouldn't have been any scratches at all. Especially since I was careful not to touch your face and neck."

"You are one crazy lady. And I still can't believe you wanted me to beat you with that gun the way I did. It just killed me to have to do that."

"Well, you did a great job, and it was very necessary. I needed the incident to look convincing, and it did. The police bought it, and so did my sister and brother-in-law."

"I guess. But it's like I told you when you first thought up this far-fetched scheme of yours, you must really want Pierce pretty badly."

"I do. I love him, Derrick, and I deserve him."

"Well, I hope you know what you're doing. And by the way," he said, sounding slightly comical, "you do realize that the man you're in love with is your sister's husband, right?"

Paige raised her eyebrows and didn't find his sarcasm very amusing. "Yeah. And?"

"*And* I think you're playing in dangerous territory. Not to mention you're staying at their house."

"Everything'll be fine. You'll see. This was all meant to be, and it was only a matter of time before Pierce and I got together, anyway."

"But what about your sister and how hurt she'll be?"

"What about your wife and how hurt *she* would be if she knew about all those affairs you've had?"

"Touché," he said, chuckling.

Paige laughed, too. "Touché indeed."

"Well, all I know is that I hope you never ask me to do anything like this again."

"I won't. Because once Pierce and I are married, I won't need favors from anyone."

"Really now? Well, I sure hope you don't think everything is going to be perfect and that you'll never have any problems."

"We won't. Pierce is a good man, and I plan to do everything I can to keep him happy."

"Well, I'm a good man, too, and though my wife has tried making me happy, it's not working."

"Then why won't you just leave her?"

"Well, for one thing, I don't love any of those other women. I love Andrea. Plus, you know what they say."

"What's that?"

"Married men who mess around rarely leave their wives."

Paige knew it wasn't worth responding to such nonsense, because even if that were true, she knew Pierce would be different.

Just then, she heard a knock on her door and wondered why Camille was back home.

"Hey, I'm going to have to go now, but call me later in the week."

"Will do. And you take care of yourself."

"I will."

Paige hung up and hoped Camille hadn't heard her conversation. "Come in."

"Hey, I'm sorry to interrupt."

"No problem."

"I just needed to talk to someone."

"Of course."

Camille sat down in the chair adjacent to Paige. "I see you're wearing one of your sweaters."

Paige glanced down at herself. "Yeah, it's finally cold enough, and you know I love hot pink. It really was kind of you to order those gifts for me."

"It was nothing."

"So, what did you wanna talk about?"

"Well, right after I dropped the kids off at school, I drove by Pierce's bank and decided to call him. But his executive assistant told me he wasn't available. Then I tried his cell, but, of course, it went to voicemail. I waited an hour and tried again, but he still wouldn't answer. So, can you call him for me?"

Paige wasn't sure what to say, but then she said, "I guess I could. But if he's not answering your call, he probably won't answer mine either."

"Maybe not. But can you at least try?"

She sounded desperate and pathetic, so Paige picked up her phone and searched through her contact list, acting as though she didn't know Pierce's number by heart. When she scrolled down to it, however, she pressed send. Paige hoped he wouldn't answer, but after the third ring, he did.

"Pierce Montgomery."

"Hey Pierce, this is Paige."

"I know who it is."

His tone was curt, and Paige hated this. "The reason I'm calling is because Camille really needs to talk to you."

"Well, I don't wanna talk to her."

Paige looked at Camille, not knowing what to tell her, but to

Paige's surprise, Camille took the phone and said, "Baby, please just listen to me. This is all a huge...Hello? Hello? Pierce? Hello?"

Tears fell down Camille's face, and Paige knew Pierce had hung up.

"Sis, I'm so sorry he won't talk to you."

"This is insane!" she said, standing up.

"Honey, I know, but why don't you give him some time? Let him have a day or two to calm down."

"No, we need to talk now before this gets too far out of hand. I need Pierce to know that I've never, ever been unfaithful to him."

Paige sat quietly, listening to Camille ranting and raving, and finally Camille left the room.

Paige couldn't stop smiling. Her mission was being accomplished, and all she had to do now was bide her time. When she heard a door slam, though, she got up and looked out of the window. Camille backed out of the driveway and sped off. Chances were, she was headed to the bank so she could try to force Pierce to see her.

But not before Paige spoke to him first, so she pressed redial and waited.

"Look, Paige," he said as soon as he answered. "I already told you, I don't want to talk to your sister."

"I know. And I'm not calling you for that. Camille isn't even here. She just left."

"Then what do you want?"

"Well, first of all, I just want to say how sorry I am that Camille has done this to you. I'm sorry for everything."

"Not sorrier than I am."

"You know I love my sister, but I could never support any woman who sleeps around on her husband. You're one of the best men I know, Pierce, and you don't deserve this."

"Tell me about it. But evidently I just wasn't good enough for Camille anymore."

"That's not true. If anything, you're *too* good for her."

Pierce didn't say anything.

Paige hoped she hadn't gone too far. "Why are you so quiet?"

"I guess I'm just a little surprised to hear you speaking so harshly against your own sister."

"I don't want to. But I'm also not going to stand up for anyone who's done something this awful."

"Well, you know what they say. It is what it is."

"So, what are you going to do?"

"I don't know yet. Right now, I'm too hurt and too numb to do anything."

"I can only imagine."

"Well, hey," he said. "I appreciate your calling me back and for understanding, but I need to get going, okay?"

"No problem. Also, there is one other thing I wanted to tell you."

"What's that?"

"I've decided to move back to my condo."

"Why? Did they find the guy who broke in on you?"

"No, but I really feel like you and Camille need your privacy."

"Regardless, I don't think it's a good idea for you to leave until they've arrested someone. It's just not safe."

"I've burdened you and Camille long enough, and my mind is made up."

"I really wish you'd reconsider."

"I appreciate everything you and Camille have done for me, but it really is time I get back to my own place and try to find some sense of normalcy again."

"Well, you know I'm only a phone call or a car ride away."

"I do."

"You take care of yourself, Paige."

"You, too, Pierce. And thanks again."

Paige pressed the end button and started gathering her things together. If she was going to lure Pierce from her sister the rest of the way, she needed to act quickly. She needed to do it from the comfort of her own home and be out of the Montgomery household by sundown.

Chapter 15

$\mathcal{P}$aige opened her trunk and placed two of her overnight bags inside of it but turned around when she saw Camille pulling into the driveway. She'd called Camille about two hours ago, letting her know she would be gone by noon, and Paige had sort of been hoping they wouldn't run into each other. Not because she felt bad about leaving, but because she didn't want to take a chance on Camille asking her to call Pierce again on her behalf. What she wanted was for Camille to accept that her marriage was over and simply get used to it.

Camille stepped out of her vehicle and closed the door. "I really wish you'd stay."

"You've been very nice, and two and a half weeks is more than enough. Plus, it's like I told you on the phone, you and Pierce need your privacy. Especially now."

"But they still haven't arrested anyone, and who's to say this guy won't come back?"

"I doubt he would do that, and to be honest, I'm just not afraid anymore. I'm ready to get back to my life and move on."

"Nonetheless, I still wish you'd change your mind. And I'll admit that part of me also wants you to stay for selfish reasons. I really need you to be my support system. Now more than I ever have."

"I'll only be a few miles away, and if you need me, I'll be here in minutes."

"It won't be the same. I have girlfriends and women who I'm pretty close with at church, but there's no one I trust more than you. There's no one I can confide in the way I can with my sister."

Paige slid her arm inside of Camille's, and they slowly walked up the custom brick sidewalk. "Look, you know I have your back, but this is a time when you and Pierce need to be alone so you can work through your issues. This has to be about you and him and no one else."

"Maybe."

"Has he called?"

"No, but when I stopped by the bank this morning, he did come out to the lobby to say he would see me at home."

Paige hoped this wasn't true, but said, "Well, at least it sounds like he's now ready to talk."

"I think he is, and as a matter of fact, he's going to leave work right before three o'clock so we can sit down and discuss things before the children get home. They won't be here until later because of PJ's game, and I've already asked Mom and Dad to bring them home when it's over."

Paige didn't like this and knew she had to do something. However, all she said was, "I'm glad to hear you guys are going to try to work this out."

"I am, too."

"I also hope Pierce realizes he should have had a lot more trust and faith in you, regardless of what anyone sent him in the mail."

"Yeah, I agree, but I have to admit, if someone sent me a stack of incriminating information about him, I'd probably believe them, too."

"I guess. Well, anyway, I'm going to keep you both in my prayers, and I know you'll soon get past this."

"Thanks, Paige," Camille said as they walked inside the house. "Because prayer is what we need most."

Paige hugged her sister and thought, *I'll be praying, all right. Praying that Pierce leaves your pitiful little behind so he can start his new life with me.*

* * *

It was four o'clock, and Paige had been home for nearly three hours. She hadn't thought so much about it while she'd been staying at her sister's, but she'd missed being in her own space. She'd missed her own bed, her own everything, and was glad she'd made the decision to return this afternoon. Of course, her two-bedroom condo wasn't nearly the size of the Montgomerys' three-story abode, but it was hers and she was comfortable here. There was no question that she'd loved seeing Pierce every day and had even loved spending time with her niece and nephew, but she was glad she no longer had to see or stomach her sister.

She went over to the sofa table and sorted through her last couple of days of mail. She shuffled one piece after another but pursed her lips when she saw an envelope from Lexus. Now she sort of wished she hadn't ended things so soon with Owen—and she wouldn't have had he not made that foolish proposal to her. He'd messed up everything, and as of this statement, she'd have to begin paying the entire bill on her own. Although maybe she could smooth things over with Owen for the time being. It was certainly a possibility and something well worth considering.

Paige opened a few more invoices, a check from a client, and a couple of business letters, but then her phone rang. It was Camille, and she was right on schedule.

"Hello."

"Oh my God, Paige," Camille said between sniffles and tears. "You won't believe what happened."

"What?"

"I just can't believe someone is doing all these terrible things."

"Camille, what are you talking about? Please tell me."

"Paige, someone sent me two dozen roses with a card that said, 'Baby, I'm so glad Pierce knows about us now, and that you've finally decided to leave him. I love you with all my soul. William.'"

"What?" Paige said, feigning disbelief and major concern. "This is crazy."

"I know, and even worse, Pierce had just gotten here when they arrived."

I know, because I'm the one who sent them. "Oh no, Camille. I'm so sorry. Is he still there?"

"No," Camille said, crying again. "And this time, he packed some of his clothing."

"So, he's moving out on you because of a few flowers?"

"Can you blame him? I mean, first it was all those email messages, and now roses?"

"But none of this makes any sense."

"No, it doesn't, and I just wish I knew who hated me enough to do something like this."

"But that's just it, Camille. You're one of the sweetest and most generous people I know, and everyone loves you. And hey, what if this isn't even about you? What if there's someone out there who is trying to get revenge on Pierce for some reason?"

"You know, you might be right. I hadn't even considered that."

"Stranger things have happened in the world, and nowadays you can't put anything past certain people. Pierce makes a lot of money, and who's to say someone at the bank isn't behind this? I mean, it could even be someone who's had it in for him for years and maybe something related to the last bank he worked at."

"But would someone go this far? And why would they specifically try to hurt me?"

"It's like I just said, maybe it's not about you."

"I just hate this, and I have no idea how I'm going to fix it."

"Just keep praying, and keep trying to talk to Pierce."

"I will."

"Do you want me to come back over?"

"No, I'm going to contact the florist to see what information I can get, and then try and call Pierce. After that, I'm going to go pick the children up and take them to spend the night at Mom and Dad's."

"Well, call me if you need me, okay?"

"I will, and thanks, Paige. For everything."

As soon as Paige hung up, she thought about calling Pierce, but decided it might be best to wait a day or two. So instead she picked up the latest Victoria's Secret catalog and carefully turned through one page at a time, checking out the various negligees and panty and bra sets she knew Pierce would adore. She saw a number of them, and since she couldn't decide on any one item over another, she would buy them all. She would go online in a few minutes, place her order, and request overnight delivery. She would do this because there was no doubt she'd be making love to Pierce any day now.

Chapter 16

*P*aige curled her legs onto the sofa, covered her body with a leopard-print blanket, and turned the channel on her television. There was absolutely nothing like watching Lifetime Movie Network, and Paige could already tell this was going to be a great movie. She liked it because the protagonist was a woman she could definitely identify with—a woman who'd made the smart decision to go after what she wanted. Like Paige, she'd decided to take the man of her dreams from some privileged wife who didn't deserve him, and Paige applauded her. She had the highest respect for the woman's courage and God-given right to be happy.

Paige watched intensely, but about forty minutes in her cell phone rang and she reached over for it. She saw the number clear as day but was almost too excited to answer. It was Pierce, and she wondered if her eyes were playing tricks on her.

She swallowed hard, took a deep breath, and answered. "Hey."

"Did I catch you at a bad time?"

Paige sat up straighter. "No, not at all. Is everything okay?"

"No, and I really needed to talk to someone. I considered calling my mom or my brother, but for now, I just think it's best not to tell them."

"I understand. But I have to be honest about something. Even though I don't agree with what Camille has done, she's still my sister, and I don't want to be caught in the middle of you guys."

"I get that, and if you don't want to talk to me, I'll respect your decision."

"I don't mind talking to you, but if Camille finds out, she'll feel as though I'm betraying her."

"I won't say a word. Camille will never know that you and I spoke."

"I hope you mean that."

"I do."

"So, what hotel are you staying at?"

"One of the Westins downtown. Not too far from my job."

"I know a couple of travel folks who might be able to get you a decent rate, and I'm glad to call them if you want."

"My hope is that I won't be here for very long, but I'll let you know."

"Sounds good."

"You know," he said, changing the subject. "I had my suspicions about your sister long before I received those email messages."

"Really?" she said, pretending Camille hadn't told her. "I had no idea."

"Well, I did. I know you and I chatted about all the time she was spending away from home, but what I didn't tell you was that I always felt like she might be messing around. The thought of it was unbearable, though, because this kind of thing seemed so unlike Camille."

"I agree."

"And then there's the fact that I've always loved every inch of her and have never once had an affair. I've never even touched another woman in the wrong way since I married her."

"I believe you, and you can't blame yourself for any of this."

"Still, I've never been more hurt in my life, and I don't understand how we got to this point."

"Maybe this is some sort of a mistake," Paige said for lack of anything better to say.

"Oh yeah? Well, email messages with dates and times don't lie."

"Maybe they're fake."

"They look authentic enough to me. And did she tell you about the flowers?"

"No, what flowers?"

"William had roses delivered to our home while I was there, and the card said something about her leaving me."

"No way. I spoke to her this afternoon, and she never said a word."

"Wait a minute. She didn't tell you?"

"No. She told me you came by this afternoon and had already left. That was it."

"Then she was definitely lying."

"About what?"

"About the flowers and how she had no idea who this William person was or how someone had gotten our address."

"Maybe she doesn't."

"No, she's lying, because if she didn't know who they came from, she would have told you about it. She would have called you as soon as I walked out the door."

Paige didn't say anything.

"Why are you quiet? Because you know I'm right?"

"Pierce, I don't think we should talk about this anymore."

"Wait a minute. You know something, don't you? I can hear it in your voice."

"Pierce, please."

"Okay, look. I know you love Camille, but I really need you to be honest with me."

"About what?"

"Camille and this William cat. Is she seeing him or not, Paige?"

"I think we'd better end this."

"Paige, come on."

"Pierce, please don't do this."

"I promise you. Our conversation will be kept completely confidential, but I really need to know."

Paige sniffled and tried mustering real tears. "She's my sister."

Pierce sighed. "I know that, and I'm sorry for placing you in such a tough position. But if Camille really is seeing this guy, don't you think I deserve to know?"

"I'm sorry, but I have to go," she said and hung up.

But only seconds passed before her brother-in-law called her back.

"Pierce, I'm begging you to please leave this alone."

"All I'm asking is that you please just do this one favor for me. Just this one time."

Paige paused for a few seconds and finally said, "Yes. She's been talking to him for months now, and then she finally started sleeping with him."

"Gosh," Pierce said. "This can't be happening."

"But I think it's over now," Paige hurried to say, trying to sound positive.

"Even if it is, the bottom line is that it happened, and Camille has been lying to me all along."

"She made a huge mistake, but I know she's sorry for it."

"Well, sorry isn't enough. Not with this."

"See, that's why I didn't want to tell you. And why did you make me betray my sister like this? My sister who means everything to me."

"I'm sorry I asked you to do that, but I'm also glad I know the truth now. I'm glad I know who and what my wife really is."

"Camille is a good person, Pierce, and you know that."

"Yeah, well, she definitely has a funny way of showing it."

He didn't comment any further, and Paige knew this painful news of hers had broken him. "Is there anything I can do?"

"No, but I do appreciate your honesty. It hurts like hell, but at least I'm not in the dark anymore."

"Are you going to be okay?" she asked.

"I hope, but regardless, I'm going to hang up now."

"I wish there was something I could do, and I hope you'll call me if you need me."

"I'll talk to you later."

"You take care of yourself."

Paige ended the call and was amazed at her luck. Not once after those flowers had been delivered had she expected Pierce to move out and into a hotel. She certainly hadn't expected him to call her this evening either. Things were falling into place rather nicely and a lot quicker than she'd planned on, but she definitely wasn't complaining. She welcomed all that was happening and looked forward to what would evolve tomorrow, the next day, and the day after that. She wouldn't seduce Pierce immediately, but she knew it was only a matter of time before he came to her willingly and innocently. He would come to her as a brother-in-law, and Paige would play the kind and sympathetic sister-in-law who only wanted the best for him. She would do everything he expected until it was time.

Chapter 17

*P*aige positioned her black Gucci sunglasses across her nose and dialed Camille.

"Hey, you on your way?" Camille asked.

"Leaving now. I should be there in about twenty minutes."

"I'm heading out, too. See you there."

Early this morning, Paige had called to see how Camille was doing, and although Camille hadn't wanted to talk in front of the children, she'd sounded very upset and had asked if Paige would meet her at their favorite café for lunch. Of course, Paige had told her yes, and was dying to know what was bothering her. Clearly it had to do with this whole marital disaster between her and Pierce, but she'd sounded like something specific had happened since yesterday.

Paige pressed the button on the console in the ceiling of her car, saw her garage door closing, and drove away. It was another gorgeous Indian summer day, and she felt good. She was happier and more content than she'd been in ages, and she knew it was all because of Pierce and how close she was to having a life with him. She'd dreamed about this for years, and now she wished she'd taken him from Camille before she married him. If she had, she wouldn't have been forced to spend the prime of her life dating men she hadn't cared about and then sitting back wondering when she'd find the perfect mate. She'd tried and tried and tried, but finally, she'd had to accept the fact that no man would ever excite her or turn her on the way Pierce did.

Paige turned on her radio, pressed the preset button for XM Satellite's Heart & Soul channel, and turned up the volume when she heard Kem's "Share My Life." It was a song from his *Intimacy* CD, and she loved it. She could listen to it over and over, and sometimes she did whenever she played the actual disc. The chorus talked about sharing your life with someone, trusting in that person, and then professing how they were all you wanted and were everything you needed. These sentiments described how she felt about Pierce exactly, and they would soon describe the way he felt about her. She would be all that he imagined in a woman, and she would please him eternally.

Paige bobbed her head to the song, sang along with it, and when it ended she turned on her compact disc player and listened to it again. Then she played more of Kem's songs, because the entire collection was remarkable. The man was truly talented and not nearly as publicized or recognized as he should have been, and while Paige hadn't considered it before, she was going to see what she could do about that. She worked hard for her clients and was very good at what she did, so maybe she could help him. Maybe she could skyrocket his career and make him as popular as some of the more well-known R&B artists. She would certainly try if he would have her, and she was planning to contact him. She wouldn't be able to do it just now, but she would connect with him as soon as she and Pierce were a couple.

When Paige pulled into the parking lot, she saw Camille waiting in her SUV and parked right next to her. She turned off the ignition, grabbed her purse, and got out of her car.

"Hey," Camille said, hugging her.

"Hey, honey," Paige said, and they strolled toward the restaurant.

"Thank you for coming, because I know you probably have a lot of work to do."

"Yeah, kind of. But that's one of the benefits of owning your own business. You can take off anytime you want."

"I guess that's true."

"Good afternoon, ladies," the fifty-something woman said when they walked in.

"Hello," the sisters said.

"Will it be just the two of you?"

"Yes," Camille answered.

"Then right this way."

Paige and Camille followed her to their table.

"Will this be okay?" the woman asked.

"This will be fine," Paige told her, pulling out her chair.

When they sat down, the hostess set menus in front of them and said, "Your waitress will be right with you."

Camille hung her leather tote on the back of her chair. "Thank you."

"You're welcome," the woman said. "Enjoy."

Paige scanned the area. "I love this place. Such great food."

"I know. I do, too."

"So, how are you?"

Camille's demeanor slightly changed. "Not good."

"I could tell something was wrong when I called you this morning."

"Well, first of all, two more email messages came from William last night, and even worse, they were in response to two messages that were sent from my account. And this time I actually saw all four of them."

Paige frowned. "Are you serious? But you never saw any of the others, did you?"

"No. So I'm not sure what that's about."

"Did you tell Pierce about them?"

"No, of course not. But I did call this computer expert, who sometimes works with the police, to see what he could figure out."

Paige kept her composure but was also a little nervous. "And?"

"They could see that the outgoing emails actually were sent from my computer, but they couldn't tell where the incoming messages were being generated from."

"Then I can see why you're so frustrated."

"No, but it's more than that."

"What?"

"Pierce called me this morning, saying that there was no sense in my lying anymore because he now knew for sure I was having an affair. Even said he had proof."

"Proof? What kind of proof?" Paige asked, but knew his *proof* had come from her when she'd lied and said Camille was messing around on him.

"I begged him to tell me, but he wouldn't."

"That's insane."

"Tell me about it, and I feel so defeated. I'm so tired of defending myself and pleading with him to believe me."

Paige held Camille's hand. "I'm sure you are, and I just wish there was something I could do," she said, repeating the same words she'd told Pierce last night before hanging up with him. They were such caring words, and she could tell from the look on Camille's face that she believed they were genuine.

"I know you do, and I love you for that," she said, squeezing Paige's hand. "But there's nothing anyone can do as long as Pierce believes what he believes."

"If you want, I can try to talk to him again."

"That's up to you, but at this point, I don't think anything is going to matter unless I can clear myself."

"Well, then that's what we'll have to work on. Finding out who really did this to you guys."

Tears rolled down both sides of Camille's face.

"Honey, please don't cry," Paige said.

Camille wiped the water away with both hands, and a young man walked up.

"Hello, ladies. I'm Jason, and I'll be your waiter."

"Hi Jason," Paige said.

"Is everything okay?" he asked, looking at Camille.

"Everything's fine," Paige answered.

"Then can I get you something to drink?"

"We'll have two lemonades."

"Coming right up. Also, just so you know, our specials for to-day include a fabulous tuna croissant, a chicken Caesar salad to die for, and a ten-ounce ribeye with creamy garlic mashed potatoes."

"Sounds good," Paige told him.

"Actually, we can order now if you want," Camille said, and Paige closed her menu.

"Sure. I'll have the chicken Caesar."

"And I'll have the tuna croissant."

"That was easy," the waiter said, smiling. "I'll get your order put in and will bring your drinks out shortly."

"Thanks," Paige said.

When the young man left, Camille breathed deeply and shook her head. "I just don't know what I'll do if my marriage is over. I don't know what the kids or I will do, because you know how much they love their father."

"You haven't told them anything, have you?"

"Not the truth. Pierce and I agreed that it was better if we simply told them he was going to be away on a business trip for a while."

"Actually, that's probably the best thing for now. And what about Mom and Dad?"

"No, because I don't wanna upset them. Plus, I'm so ashamed."

"Yeah, but you didn't do anything," Paige said, although she was glad Camille hadn't told their parents the news, because this way her evil mother wouldn't suspect that Paige was up to anything.

After the waiter brought their food, they ate, but Camille didn't say very much. Now they were finished and ready to pay the check.

"I'll get this," Paige said, taking the slip of paper from her sister.

"You don't have to do that."

"You pay all the time, so please let me do this."

"Okay, if you insist," Camille said, placing her wallet back inside her bag.

"I do."

"Thank you again for meeting me."

"No problem, and if you want me to drop by later I will."

"I think I'm going to take the kids out to dinner, but I'll call you if I change my mind."

Paige took care of the bill, and they went outside.

"I'll see you later," Camille said as they hugged.

"I love you," Paige said. "And please don't ever forget that."

"I won't. I love you, too."

Paige got into her car, dialed Pierce's cell phone, and waved goodbye to her sister.

"Hello?" he said.

"Hey, I know you're working, so I won't keep you. But how are you today?"

"Hurt. Angry. Stunned. You name it."

"I could tell how upset you were last night, and that's why I wanted to call and check on you."

"Have you spoken to Camille?" he asked.

"Yeah, we just had lunch."

"I'm glad to hear she's going on with business as usual."

"Maybe you should try to call her."

"I don't even wanna hear Camille's voice, and I certainly don't wanna see her. I do miss my kids, though, and it's killing me to be without them."

"I'm sure they miss you, too."

Paige waited for him to respond but when he didn't she continued. "Like I said, I know you're at work, so I'll just check on you tomorrow."

"Thanks, Paige. You take care now."

"You, too."

Paige dropped her BlackBerry onto the passenger seat, slipped her sunglasses back on, and zipped out of the parking lot. It was only two o'clock, but by golly, her work was already done for the day. Boy was she good.

Chapter 18

$\mathcal{P}$aige separated her whites, darks, lights, and towels into four different piles and poured liquid detergent into the washer. Then she added a full scoop of powdered OxiClean and the appropriate amount of fabric softener and tossed in all her white clothing. She turned the washer on, closed the top of it, and went back into the kitchen. She'd eaten lunch with Camille about five hours ago, but she was starting to get hungry again.

Poor, poor Camille and all the trouble she was dealing with. Having an affair, lying about it, and then trying to figure out what she and her children were going to do now that Pierce was gone. If things had been different between them, and Paige had loved her the way most sisters actually loved each other, she might feel sorry for her. But the truth of the matter was, she didn't. She did care about Camille, she guessed, and she loved her niece and nephew for sure, but she couldn't and wouldn't allow Pierce to go back to them. She couldn't let him slip through her fingers after all the hard work she'd put in, not to mention all the waiting she'd done. Plus, PJ and Crystal would be fine. They would still have an extremely close relationship with their father and would go on to be very happy children, once they saw that their father was better off with their auntie.

Paige went into the living room and turned on Kem's CD and then walked back into the kitchen. She opened the refrigerator, pulled out a head of lettuce, an onion, a tomato, mayo, ketchup, and a package of Jennie-O ground turkey patties. She loved almost anything made of turkey, but this particular ninety-three percent fat-free version with natural seasonings was her favorite.

She turned on one of the burners, pulled a nonstick saucepan from the cabinet, sprayed it with butter-flavored Pam, and opened a package of whole wheat buns. She pulled one of them out, placed both halves in the skillet, and let them brown for a few minutes. Then she removed the buns, set them on a plate, and sprayed them with fat-free butter spray. This product really did taste like real butter, and she was so glad Karla had suggested she switch from one of the other brands to this one. Finally, she placed her turkey burger in the skillet and cut up her veggies. It wouldn't take more than ten minutes or so for it to cook all the way through, so Paige leaned against the counter, thinking. She thought about how neat it was going to be once she was finally able to fix meals for Pierce. It would be such a joy, having a reason to prepare all the complicated recipes she'd been wanting to try. Of course, Camille was a pretty good cook, too, and Paige quickly gave credit when it was due, but she wasn't better than Paige. Camille even admitted it herself, so this was yet another way Paige would be able to satisfy Pierce more favorably.

When her burger was ready, Paige melted a slice of lowfat cheese on it, removed it with a spatula, and placed it on the bun. As soon as she did, her doorbell rang. She wasn't expecting anyone but grinned when she realized it might be Pierce and rushed to the door.

Unfortunately, it wasn't him.

"What do you want?" she said and Owen brushed past her without being invited in.

"Is that any way to talk to the man who loves you? The man who was interrogated by the police and willingly gave them a DNA sample? The man who still wants to marry you?"

"I can't believe you came by here without calling," she said, closing the door.

"Oh, so now I need to ask permission?"

Paige sighed and went back into the kitchen.

"You're too much," he said, following her. "So, I guess I don't even exist now."

"I was just about to have dinner, Owen, so what is it you want?"

"The same thing I've always wanted. For you to be my wife."

Paige took a bite of her sandwich and wished he'd leave her alone.

"So, you're not going to say anything?" he asked.

"What is there to say?"

"A lot."

"I don't think so."

"Okay, look, baby. I'm sorry I came over here unannounced, but I can't help how I feel. I'm in love with you, Paige."

As hungry as Paige had been, her appetite suddenly vanished. "Owen, we've already been through all of this. The night you proposed and then again a few days later."

"I know," he said, moving in front of her. "But I really wish you'd reconsider."

Paige sniffed her nose a couple of times and frowned. "Have you been drinking?"

"Well, if I have, it's because of you."

"Owen, I'd really like you to leave."

"No. I'm not leaving until I get what I came for. I won't go until you agree to marry me."

His words were a bit slurred, and Paige didn't like where this impromptu visit was going.

"Owen, I'm sorry things didn't work out between you and me, but you and I are over."

"You lowdown trick."

Paige raised her eyebrows. "Excuse me?"

"You heard me. You lowdown, connivin', schemin' trick. You used me and played me like some childish knucklehead, and I want back every dime I spent on you."

"You must be out of your mind."

Owen grabbed both of her arms, squeezing them with all his might.

"Owen, stop it! You're hurting me."

"I'm not playing with you, Paige. I want my money, and I'm not leaving here until I get it."

"Let me go!" she said, trying to escape, but she couldn't.

"Give me my money, and I will."

"I said, let me go!" she demanded, and this time she broke free. "You're nuts."

Owen looked at her with glazed eyes and left the kitchen.

Paige rushed behind him. "Where are you going?"

Owen kept walking until he entered her bedroom.

"Owen, get out of here or I'm calling the police."

"Go ahead," he said, snatching her purse from the bed, unzipping it, and tossing out every item inside of it.

"What in the world are you doing?"

Owen ignored her and opened her wallet. "Is this all you have?" he said, pulling out four twenties. "Well, at least that's a start." Then he pulled out a folded picture. "Whoaaaa, now what do we have here?"

"Give it to me," she said, desperately reaching for it.

"No," he said, slightly staggering. "Now, why would you have a photo of you, your sister, and your brother-in-law with your sister's face crossed out in black marker? And why is there a heart drawn next to Pierce?"

"That's none of your business," Paige said, still trying to recover her property.

"I thought you and your sister were close."

"We are, and you know it."

"Doesn't look that way to me. No, what this looks like is you hating your sister. It also looks like you have some sort of infatuation with your brother-in-law."

"You're sick."

"No, I don't think so, and maybe this is the real reason you don't want me."

Paige snatched the photo from him, hurried back into the kitchen, and grabbed her phone.

But Owen charged after her, half staggering again, and took it away from her. "You're not callin' anybody."

"You're drunk," she said and thanked God her phone rang.

Owen blinked a couple of times. "Now, let's see who we have here."

"Give me my phone, Owen."

"Hello?" he said. "Sure, she's right here, Karla. And how have you been doing?...Good...So have I. Well, actually, that's a lie, because I just found out your girl here hates her sister and has a crush on her husband. But I'll let her tell you about that."

Paige grabbed the phone. "Girl, Owen is over here acting like a madman."

"What?"

"Yes, so will you please call the police?"

"Okay, I'm goin'," he said, walking toward the kitchen doorway. "But I'm tellin' you now. I want every dime of my money, or I'll have to tell your sister what I saw."

"Owen, please go."

"No problem. Oh, and I hope you don't forget what I told you the other day. People should be very careful when they play with other people's emotions."

Paige stared at him, and thankfully, he left.

"Girl, Owen is crazy," she told Karla. "First he came over here without calling, and then he started rantin' and ravin' about all the money he's spent on me. He's so pissed off because I won't marry him."

"After hearing him like this, I guess so. And what in heaven's name was he talking about when he brought up Camille and Pierce?"

"I don't have a clue, and I don't think he does either. He practically reeked with alcohol."

"Geez. He almost sounds like some kind of fatal attraction."

"I hope not," Paige said, even though Owen *was* starting to worry her. He was acting way out of character and not like the man she'd known for many months.

"Still, I think you should take every precaution, and if he bothers you again, I would call the police and file an order of protection."

"Hopefully, he won't be back and won't ever call me again."

"Man, I guess you never know people, do you? The Owen I met always seemed so nice."

"Yeah, I thought the same thing until now."

"Are you sure you're okay?"

"I will be."

"Do you want me to come over?"

"Do you mind?"

"Of course not."

"Thanks, Karla."

"See you soon."

Paige was glad Karla was coming by, but what troubled her was that photo Owen had spotted. How could she have been so stupid, carrying such a tell-all item in her wallet and risking someone seeing it? But what had been the odds of Owen bursting into her room and searching through her personal property? She hoped he was planning to keep his mouth shut. Although since he was noticeably intoxicated, there was a chance he wouldn't even remember.

This was the most Paige could hope for, anyway.

Chapter 19

$\mathcal{T}$J, one of the morning anchors on CNN, gave a rundown of what they'd be covering at the top of the hour, and Paige revved up her treadmill. She hadn't used it since the morning of her "rape," and she was starting to feel the effects. She hadn't gained any noticeable weight, but she felt sluggish and like her tummy wasn't as flat as usual. So she was glad to be back on track and working up a heavy sweat the way she should.

Paige pumped her arms and strode at a speed of 4.8 miles per hour and thought about Owen. She'd tried to push the idea of his seeing that photo completely from her mind, but she hadn't been able to. She'd tossed and turned and tossed and turned again, until finally she'd found herself up surfing the Internet until three a.m. She'd almost been tempted to call him just to see if he'd bring it up, but then she'd figured it might not be a good idea since he likely wasn't sober yet.

Everything had been going so well for her when it came to Pierce, but now Owen gave her plenty of reason to worry. He hadn't taken the photo with him, and not long after he'd left, she'd torn it into a hundred pieces, but if he still remembered what he'd seen, his words could certainly do damage. They would ease suspicion into Camille's mind, and while she wouldn't want to believe him, she might start second-guessing Paige and suspecting something was wrong. She might begin piecing things together and would soon discover that the problems in her marriage hadn't started until after Paige had moved in with them. Sure, she'd changed the outgoing times on some of those email messages, so it would seem there was no way she could have sent them. But at the same time, Camille might begin doubting her, and Paige couldn't have that. At least not yet, anyway, and she prayed to God that this would pass and not become an issue.

When Paige finished her full sixty minutes, she did a five-minute cool-down, went into the kitchen, and grabbed a bottle of water. She drank the entire sixteen ounces and was thinking about having another when her phone rang. It was only seven o'clock, so she wondered who was calling so early. She was relieved and ecstatic, however, when she saw it was Pierce.

"Hey, how's it goin'?" she said between breaths.

"Is everything okay?" he asked.

"Everything's great. Just finished working out is all."

"Oh. Well, I know it's early, but I really need to ask you something."

"Of course."

"Are you absolutely positive that Camille has been having an affair?"

Paige wondered why he was questioning what she'd told him. "I'm very positive. But why do you ask?"

"Because I guess it's still so hard for me to believe Camille would do something like this and keep a straight face the whole time she was seeing this man."

"I understand that, and I know this has to be very difficult to fathom, but Pierce, please know that I would never, ever lie on my sister. Although now I regret telling you anything. I knew it was wrong, and I should have stayed out of it."

"No, I'm glad you did tell me, but it's tough when someone just ups and becomes a totally different person than what you've known all these years."

Paige listened quietly.

"But," he continued, "I do know one thing. You of all people would never make up something like this."

"No, I wouldn't. I'm just not that kinda person."

"There is one other thing, though. Camille told me that a number of those emails were sent at times when she wasn't even home."

Paige had known it was only a matter of time before Camille finally paid attention to detail. Especially since she was desperate and looking for anything she could that might prove her innocence.

"I don't want to say anything against my sister, but you know as well as I do that any of us can access our email accounts from any computer we want. Anytime, anyplace."

"Yeah, I know. Anyway, I won't keep you, and I promise not to bother you about this anymore."

"It's really not a problem. Everyone needs someone to talk to when they're going through the kind of thing you're dealing with."

"Very true."

"So, will you see PJ and Crystal this weekend?"

"Yes, and since I now know for sure that I won't be moving back home for a while, if ever, I'm going to tell Camille it's time we sit down and explain things to them. I need to do it before I leave on Sunday for a banking conference next week in Vegas."

"Wait a minute. You're going to Vegas on Sunday?"

"Yes."

"Wow, now this is too weird, because I'm going there on Monday. One of my clients has two major media interviews on both

Tuesday and Wednesday and then a seminar he's speaking at on Thursday."

"Oh really?"

"What a coincidence, huh?" she said.

"That's for sure."

"So, where are you staying?"

"The Palazzo. What about you?"

"The Venetian," she said, remembering Karla had stayed there in the past.

"That's right next door, so maybe we can have dinner or at least a drink one evening."

"Maybe," she said, trying to sound uninterested. "It'll depend on how much time I'll need to spend with my client, since I'm still pitching other media outlets."

"Of course. Business comes first, so we'll just play it by ear."

"Hey, it looks like I have another call," she said, making an excuse so she could hang up and begin making her travel arrangements. "But I really hope you get to spend some quality time with the children."

"Thanks, and I'll talk to you later."

Paige held the phone against her chest with both hands and shouted with joy. This was all too good to be true, and while she'd had no plans whatsoever of being in Vegas or in any other city on business next week, she was glad she'd been quick on her toes. The lie had entered her mind and eased out of her mouth so naturally. She hadn't stuttered or hesitated in the slightest bit before telling Pierce she would be heading to Nevada one day after he was. She hadn't even had to think before speaking, so she knew this trip was meant to be.

Paige zoomed into her extra bedroom, which was actually her office, and pulled up The Palazzo's website. She knew she'd told Pierce she was staying at The Venetian, and if he asked her why she'd changed her mind, she would simply tell him that since he'd mentioned The Palazzo and she'd never stayed there before or even been to Vegas (which was true), she'd decided to check it out. Also, now that she'd had a chance to read some of the hotel information, she could see that The Palazzo was newer than The Venetian, so that was even more reason to give it a try.

Paige browsed The Palazzo website and saw that it housed suites only and that the prices were determined by square footage. Of course, she would need to go with the smallest and most economical one, which was the Palazzo Luxury Suite at seven hundred twenty square feet, but that was more than enough room for her. As she read down the list, though, she was willing to bet Pierce was likely staying in either The Palazzo Fortuna or The Palazzo Sienna, which were nine hundred forty and one thousand two hundred eighty square feet, respectively. They were huge, and if Paige got her way, she'd be hanging out in one of those big boys with him.

After reserving the hotel, she searched for the best flight prices and was floored when she saw that the lowest available was just over seven hundred dollars. She knew it was because of last-minute booking, but it wasn't as though she had other options. Not when she needed to be in Las Vegas Monday through Friday. So, if the fare had been two thousand, she would have maxed out one of her credit cards to purchase it.

When she'd chosen her flight times, selected her seats, and paid for her ticket, she thought about Camille and called her.

"Hey, sis," Paige said. "How are you?"

"Okay, I guess. What about you?"

"I'm fine, but I was sitting here trying to remember if I told you I had to travel next week."

"No, where are you going?"

"I guess with everything that's been going on, I forgot. Anyway, you know my speaking client, right?"

"Yeah."

"Well, he has media and events in New York, so I'm going to meet him there on Monday."

"I haven't been to New York in years, and wish I could go with you."

"I wish you could, too." *But it'll never happen, sweetheart.*

"I would, but Pierce will be at a conference out in Vegas all next week. It's been planned for a couple of months, and I don't want to leave PJ and Crystal."

"I understand. So, have you spoken to Pierce this morning?"

"I actually just hung up with him not long ago, but things aren't good."

"Why?"

"He's decided to stay at his hotel indefinitely, and he wants us to tell the children."

"Gosh, Camille, this whole thing really breaks my heart, but I gotta believe Pierce will eventually come around. Either the truth will come out or he'll just forgive you at some point and you'll be back together in no time."

"We'll see."

"You sound so down."

"That's because this is the hardest and most painful thing I've ever had to deal with, and I'm so out of sorts. I'm in tears all the time, I can't sleep, and the thought of losing the only man I've ever truly loved terrifies me."

"I just don't know what to say," Paige said.

"I don't either, and I'm so worried about Crystal and PJ and how they're going to react to our splitting up."

"Well, you know I'll be there for all three of you as soon as I get back."

"I know, and I'm depending on that, Paige."

"You have my word."

They chatted for a few minutes longer, and while Paige wished she could care about her sister's sorrow, she thought more about Pierce and the fabulous time they would have out West. She even thought about those amazing pieces she'd ordered from Victoria's Secret and how they'd been delivered yesterday right on schedule. Pierce would be in complete awe, and they would make love like it was their only opportunity.

They would have the time of their lives and would start preparing for their wonderful new beginning.

Chapter 20

*R*ight after Paige hung up with Karla, making sure she understood how busy Paige was going to be on her business trip—and that she wouldn't be able to talk to her very much at all this week—Paige parked inside O'Hare's multilevel ramp. Then she got out of her car, removed her luggage, and headed toward the elevator. Once she stepped inside of it and pressed the terminal button, the door closed and she realized she was that much closer to Las Vegas. When she arrived upstairs at the check-in terminals, she swiped her credit card, waited for her reservation information to display, and followed the instructions. To her surprise, a first-class upgrade offer appeared on the screen, and she quickly accepted it. The cost was only one hundred fifty dollars, and she was ecstatic over it. Camille and Pierce flew first-class regularly and loved it, so she always tried upgrading as often as she could, too.

After she received her boarding pass and made it through security, preparing to walk to her departing gate, her phone rang. It was Derrick, calling from his office.

"Hey, D," she said in a chipper tone.

"Hey, how's it goin'?"

"Great. On my way to sunny Las Vegas."

"Really? For what?"

"To be with Pierce, of course."

"Excuse me?"

"He's there on business this week."

"And he invited you to come stay with him?"

"Not exactly. But when I told him I was going to be there with one of my clients for a few days, anyway, he said we should try to have dinner or drinks."

Derrick cracked up. "Okay, but let me guess. There's no *client* anywhere near Vegas, right?"

"Of course there isn't. But Pierce doesn't know that."

"You're too much," Derrick said, laughing more intensely. "First you fake being raped so you could move in with them, and now this."

Paige didn't see anything funny.

"So, you're actually going to try to lure this man into bed, aren't you?"

"You make it sound so pathetic."

"Well, it kind of is."

"I thought you were my friend, Derrick."

"I am, and that's why I'm so concerned and wish you wouldn't do this."

"Then why did you help me that night? Because you knew full well that the only reason I had to resort to something so outrageous was because I couldn't find any other way to ruin Camille and Pierce's marriage."

"I helped you because you threatened to tell Andrea about all of my affairs, remember? Not to mention, I felt like I owed you for all those times you let me bring certain women to your condo. But now that I see how obsessed you are with taking your sister's husband, I regret everything I did."

"Obsessed?" Paige said a little too loudly, and the woman

walking in front of her turned around and looked at her. "Who's obsessed?"

"You are, Paige. You're taking this thing way too far, and as God is my witness, no good is going to come from it."

"I disagree, and that's why I'm going to do everything in my power to be with the man I love."

"I wish you'd reconsider."

"Not gonna happen."

"I hate to hear that."

Paige sighed. "Look, Derrick, I know you're worried, but I promise you, everything is going to be fine. So why can't you just be happy for me?"

"Because I know a disaster waiting to happen when I see one."

"I'm sorry you feel that way."

"I'm sorry you won't listen to me."

"Hey, all I'm doing is living out my destiny. I'm doing what everyone in the world should do before it's too late."

Derrick didn't say anything, so she said, "I think I'm gonna grab a latte, so I'd better go now."

"Take care of yourself, Paige."

"Count on it."

* * *

Paige stored her laptop bag in the overhead bin and sat in the third row next to the window. She knew it would be a while before those seated in coach finished loading, so she decided this would be a good time to call Camille. It was the perfect time to talk about her fabricated trip to New York and how excited she was to be going there.

"Hey, honey," Camille said when she answered.

"Hey, how are you?"

"Okay, I guess. Are you on your way to New York?"

"On the plane now. I'm so looking forward to it and wish you were going, so we could spend some time on Fifth Avenue together."

"I do, too, but I know you'll have a wonderful time."

"I know I will. And how are the children?"

"Not great. We told them about the separation, and it didn't go over too well."

"I'm sure the news must have been very shocking and painful for them, but the good thing is that children are very resilient. More so than adults even."

"I hope that's true, and interestingly enough, PJ is the one who is taking this the hardest, even though he's the oldest."

"Yeah, but that's sort of understandable because he's always been a Daddy's boy."

"He has, and I'm sure that's why he's so upset. He cried most of Saturday."

Paige casually flipped through the airline magazine she'd just pulled from the seat pocket in front of her. "You know, as much as I hate saying this, I don't know if I'll ever be able to look at Pierce the same, because what man leaves his wife and children over a few petty email messages and a flower delivery?"

"He left because he says he has proof," Camille said in a disheartened tone. "He was already upset and believing I was having an affair, but when he received whatever proof he's talking about, that's when he turned completely cold toward me. That's when he completely shut down and decided he wasn't coming home."

Paige looked up when she saw a flight attendant approaching her and was glad she had an excuse to end this depressing phone call.

"Hey, sis, I hate to cut this short, but I have to go now. I'll call you this evening, though."

"Okay. You have a safe flight."

"Thanks, I will. Love you."

"I love you, too."

Paige set her phone on her lap.

"Can I get you something to drink?" the flight attendant asked.

"Just ice water, please."

"No problem."

Paige leaned back in the spacious leather seat and relaxed. There was nothing like flying first-class or being treated like a first-class person. Life just didn't get any better than this, and once she married Pierce, she'd fly this way from here on out. Not as a result of some random last-minute upgrade offer. She would do so because Pierce could afford it.

Paige exhaled with the utmost relief—until her phone rang and Owen's name displayed on her screen. He was the last person she wanted to speak to, but she also didn't think it was in her best interest to ignore him.

"Hello?"

"You got my money yet?"

"No."

"Well, I suggest you get it, because if you don't, I'll have to tell your sister about that photo you're carrying around and drooling over."

"Tell her what you want," Paige said, knowing she didn't mean that.

"Fine with me. Talk to you later."

"No, wait," she hurried and said.

"Yes?" he sneered.

"I'll get you your money when I'm back in town."

"From where? And when?"

"Where is none of your business, but I'll be back this week-end."

"I'll call you on Saturday," he said and hung up.

This thing with Owen wasn't good, and while she didn't have the kind of cash he'd spent on her, she knew she had to figure out a way to pay him. She had to fix this before Owen did something stupid and ruined everything.

Chapter 21

After landing at McCarran International Airport and passing one slot machine after another, Paige picked up her luggage, lined up for a taxi, and was on her way to the hotel. She was stunned by the number of people who loved, loved, loved gambling and would sell their souls to the devil if they thought it would help them strike it rich, and she was glad she didn't fall into that category. She was glad she didn't have an addictive or obsessive bone in her body.

When the driver pulled up to The Palazzo, she paid him, told the bellman she was fine handling her own garment bag on wheels, and then went inside the alluring, artistically designed lobby. The Palazzo was all she'd hoped it would be, and she felt right at home already.

She walked up to the registration desk, waited a couple of minutes for her room assignment, thanked the guest services representative for placing her on one of the highest floors, and went on her way. During her trip to the elevators, however, she'd strolled through a massive casino, looking at hundreds of colorful machines and a few blackjack tables, and then saw a security guard sitting just in front of the elevator hallway. She wondered why he was there, but then she saw others flashing their room keys, proving that they were in fact Palazzo guests. She did the same, the handsome guard nodded with approval, and she smiled and proceeded up to her suite.

As soon as she arrived, she walked in and toured the place she would call home until Friday. The marble vanity and polished floors in the bathroom were unbelievable, as were the exquisite bedding and draperies, and she loved the sitting-area furniture, which was more appealing than what she'd decorated her condo with. Everything about this space was mesmerizing, and she wished she could stay here for weeks. But truth was, all she needed was a day or so to seduce Pierce.

Paige unpacked her clothing, hung it up, spread out her toiletries in the bathroom, and called her brother-in-law. His phone rang four times and went into voicemail, but before she could leave a message, she heard her call waiting signal. It was Pierce calling back.

"So, are you here?" he asked.

"Yep. I just checked in."

"Did you have a good flight?"

"I did. No delays and no turbulence."

"Good. Well, if you're not too tired, maybe we could have dinner tonight? Or we could try tomorrow night as well."

"Tonight is fine."

"Okay, then why don't you meet me at SushiSamba. It's a fabulous Japanese restaurant I enjoy."

"I love Japanese."

"Is seven okay?"

"That's perfect."

"I'll see you then."

Paige ended the call, went straight to the closet, and pulled out her favorite dress. She held it against her body, admiring herself in the full-length mirror, and had no doubt Pierce would be pleased. He would take a second, third, and maybe even a fourth look before gathering his composure, and he wouldn't be able to stop himself from lusting over her. He'd be tempted to skip dinner and take her back to his suite as fast as he could, but she wouldn't let him. No, what she would do was listen to whatever he had to say with maximum interest—she would bond with him the way any two people should whenever they were officially trying to get to know each other. After that, though, she'd become more flirtatious and attentive without him realizing it, and soon they'd be on their way out of the restaurant. In minutes, they'd be in his room and in his bed making love like wild animals, and there would be no turning back. They would be connected from this day forward the way Paige had planned.

Chapter 22

*P*aige entered The Palazzo Shoppes area where the restaurant was located and wished she could buy a few items from Barneys New York. She also passed by MaxMara, Charriol, and a men's store called Billionaire Italian Couture and decided right then that the next time she and Pierce came to Las Vegas, she would buy him multiple gifts from there.

As she walked farther along, she saw Pierce standing and waiting for her. Gosh, did this man look good, all dressed in a navy blue suit and a snow white French-cuffed shirt. He must have removed his tie for the evening, and Paige liked the semicasual yet still very classy appearance it gave him. But then she looked pretty good herself, so they were even. Paige wore a tailor-fitted red sheath dress with diamond earrings and a diamond bracelet, both of which she was still paying for, and her hair was twisted upward in an elegant knot. To complete her outfit, she wore the most beautiful four-inch black, pointed-toe pumps she'd seen in a while and was glad she'd purchased them a couple of hours ago. When she'd gone down to the Forum Shops at Caesars Palace, she hadn't planned on buying anything, but as soon as she'd spotted these particular shoes, she'd known they'd be ideal for tonight and that she had to have them.

"Hey, sister-in-law," Pierce said, eyeing her from head to toe and hugging her.

"Hey."

"Our table is ready, but I figured I'd wait for you out here," he said, moving closer to the entrance.

"Are you all set, Mr. Montgomery?" a young woman asked.

"Yes, thank you."

Pierce held out his hand, allowing Paige to walk in front of him, and when they sat down at their candlelit table, the hostess placed menus in front of them. Paige thanked her and glanced around the place. The main lighting source was dim, which suited Paige just fine, and the overall ambiance was simply romantic. It was the ultimate setting for two people who would be making love for the very first time.

"So, how was your first day at the conference?" she asked.

"Long, but very productive."

"I'm glad, because sometimes these things can be pretty boring."

"Don't I know it. But this one is well worth everyone's time. And what about you? Do you have a pretty busy media schedule tomorrow with your client?"

"I do," she said. "He has a noon news TV interview and a couple of radio interviews in the afternoon."

"Well, at least you don't have to get up bright and early."

"No, but I do want to meet him over at the station about an hour or so before."

Just then, their waiter walked up and recited the night's specials. They both ordered mojitos made of Cruzan rum, mint, lime, and fresh fruit, and Pierce also ordered a couple of pieces of yellowtail sushi, but Paige passed. When the man left, there was a noticeable and awkward silence between them and all that could be heard was the instrumental music playing in the background. So Paige said, "This really is a nice place."

"Yeah, I love it. Come at least a couple of times whenever I'm in Vegas."

"I can see why."

"And how's your room over at The Venetian?"

Paige had hoped the subject of where she was staying wouldn't come up, but since it had, she said, "Well, actually, I'm staying here."

"Oh, okay," he said, clearly looking surprised.

"Yeah . . . after you mentioned The Palazzo to me the other day, I went and checked out their website. Then, after I saw how beautiful the suites were, I couldn't help booking one of them."

"I don't blame you, because it really is a great hotel."

"I'm definitely glad I made the switch."

"So, did you speak to your sister today?" he asked, suddenly changing the subject, and Paige wished he'd forget about Camille.

"I did. Right before my plane took off. Did you?"

"No. I spoke to PJ and Crystal, though, before they went to school."

"Camille told me PJ is really upset."

"He is. He's hurt, angry, and doesn't understand why his mom and I have separated."

"I'm sure, and I'll be honest with you, Pierce. I'm not sure I'll ever be able to look at Camille the same after what she's done," she commented, knowing she'd told Camille the same thing about Pierce a few hours ago. "I mean, she's my sister, and yes, I still love her, but she's so wrong for this."

There was more silence between them, so Pierce browsed through the menu. Paige did the same and was happy when the waiter brought their drinks.

"Are you ready to order?" he asked.

"Paige?" Pierce said.

"Um...I think I'll have the causa de langosta," she said, referring to their main lobster entrée, which was poached in a pisco
rocoto butter sauce.

"And you, sir?"

"I'll have the twenty-ounce bone-in ribeye."

"Excellent choice. Very tasty."

"Also, what do you have with vodka in it?" Pierce continued,
and Paige was a little surprised, because in the past whenever
she'd gone out to nice restaurants with him and Camille, she'd
never seen either of them order more than one drink, and usually
that was only a glass of wine.

"Hmmm," the waiter said, thinking for a second. "I'd recom-
mend our niña fresa."

Pierce closed his menu. "Sounds good to me," he said, but
when the waiter left he looked at Paige. "Sure you don't want anything else to drink?"

"Positive. And if you don't mind my saying so, I'm a bit
shocked to see *you* ordering another one."

Pierce drank the last few drops of his first cocktail and said,
"You'd be amazed at what pain and disappointment will cause a
person to start doing."

Paige wasn't sure how to respond and thought it was best to
say nothing. They did eventually chat about politics and the econ-
omy, and when the waiter brought out their meals, they dug in.
Although, after eating a few bites of his steak and a couple of fork-
fuls of potatoes, Pierce ordered a third drink and then a fourth.
At the moment, he seemed extremely relaxed and ready for just
about anything.

"You know," he said, sipping more of his latest drink, the
one he'd requested double vodka in. "You really look beautiful
tonight."

"So do you."

"Actually, I've always thought that about you."

"Really? Well, you've never said it."

"Yeah, well, it's not like a married man can just go around saying something like that to another woman. Especially in front of his wife."

"No, I guess not."

"You're a good sister-in-law, Paige, and I'm glad you're here."

Paige noticed the same glaze in Pierce's eyes that she'd seen last week in Owen's, and she knew he was pretty tipsy and borderline drunk.

"This was great," she said, glancing at her watch. "But I think I'm gonna head up to my suite to do a little work. What about you? Do you have to be up pretty early?"

"The conference starts at nine."

"Then you'd better get to bed."

"I know."

Pierce charged the bill to his room, but only after pulling out his key card envelope to see what suite he was staying in. He'd had so much to drink, he couldn't fully remember.

When they left the restaurant and turned the corner, Pierce stopped and said, "Whoa, I think I had a little too much."

Paige chuckled. "I *know* you did, which is why I'd better make sure you get to your room without problems."

Pierce smiled, placed his arm around her shoulders, trying to steady himself, and they went on their way. When they walked in front of his double-door suite, however, Pierce fumbled with the key, so Paige took it and inserted it properly. Once inside, she turned on the entryway light and then helped him into the bedroom. It was just as she'd thought: Pierce had reserved a Sienna suite, which was larger than some apartments she'd been in.

Paige slid off his suit jacket, and without warning, Pierce burst into tears. He cried like a baby and hugged her for dear life.

"This hurts so, so much," he said. "I wish it didn't, and I wish I could just get past it, but I can't. I can't stop thinking about the way Camille betrayed me, and all I want is for this pain to end. Do you understand that, Paige?" he said, gazing into her eyes. "Do you have any idea how hard this is?"

Paige knew her opportunity had finally come, and she took it. "I think I do," she said, hugging him close again. They stood cheek to cheek, but Paige slowly moved her face just enough so their lips met. She kissed him softly and said, "I'm so sorry, Pierce, but I'm here for you from now on. You hear me?"

Pierce stroked her hair back with both his hands and kissed her zealously and forcefully. He acted as though he'd been waiting for a chance to be with her for years and like he hadn't been with any woman in months.

They kissed and moaned, and Pierce unzipped Paige's dress. Paige unbuttoned his shirt, removed his cuff links, and slid his shirt down his arms. They were drenched with raging passion, and Paige's body flamed with desire.

She pushed him onto the bed, slid off his pants and underwear, and then slipped out of her own. She could immediately see how ready he was for her, so she gave him what he wanted. She would do other things too—anything that would satisfy him and make him forget about her sister.

Chapter 23

Paige opened her eyes, gazed at the ceiling, and saw Pierce sitting on the side of the bed. He was wearing a complimentary plush white Palazzo robe, and she hoped he would shed it any time now.

Paige smiled and stretched her body. "Good morning."

"Morning," he said but didn't turn and look at her.

She glanced at the clock and saw that it was six o'clock. "So, how long have you been awake?"

"A while."

Paige sat up, got on her knees, and slithered across the bed behind him. Then she rested her hands on his shoulders, preparing to give him a massage. But Pierce moved away from her, stood up, and held both sides of his forehead.

"What's wrong?" she asked, confused.

"Everything."

"I know, baby, but now that you and I are together, Camille won't ever be able to hurt you again. Things are going to be very different."

Pierce finally locked eyes with her. "Look, Paige. What happened last night was a huge mistake, and I'll never be able to forgive myself. I never should have let something like this happen."

Paige's heart plummeted. "You don't mean that."

"I do, and I'm so ashamed."

"But if this wasn't supposed to happen, it never would have. Right?"

"I allowed it to happen, and now I'll have to live with that decision for the rest of my life. I got drunk, but I knew what I was doing, and I knew why."

"What do you mean?" Paige asked, panicking.

"I wanted revenge. I wanted to hurt Camille the same way she hurt me."

"I don't believe that."

"I did, Paige, and I'm so sorry this thing happened between you and me, because I know how much you love your sister."

"*Thing?*"

"Yes, this whole unfortunate thing that we both now regret."

Paige's heart raced. "Pierce, baby, please don't feel that way," she said, leaving the bed and walking over to him with nothing on. Pierce passed her a robe just like the one he was wearing and Paige reluctantly took it and wrapped it around herself.

Pierce moved closer to the window overlooking the Strip. "God, what in the world was I thinking?"

"You were thinking that you wanted to finally be happy. You did what your heart told you to do, and there's nothing wrong with that."

"Yeah, but I did it for the wrong reasons. I acted irrationally, and for the first time since I married Camille, I was unfaithful to her. Fifteen years of marriage, and in one night, I did the worst thing imaginable."

"But only because she's been doing the same thing to you for months."

"Still, as the saying goes, two wrongs don't make a right, and you and I both know that."

Paige stood next to him. "True. I'll give you that. But now it's time you and I move on. I do love my sister, and I feel terrible about what I've done to her, but Pierce . . . I don't regret what happened. Last night was amazing. I mean, we actually made love, and it felt so, so good. It was absolutely incredible."

Pierce left her standing at the window. "Paige, what you and I did was have sex. We both lost control, and it can never happen again."

Paige swallowed hard. "You just need time. You need time to end things with Camille and find closure. Then you and I can work on our new life together."

Pierce frowned. "You're not serious?"

"Of course I am."

"No, you couldn't be."

Paige took a seat on the side of the bed again. "Okay, Pierce, I guess I need to be honest with you. So can you please come sit next to me for a few minutes?"

At first he hesitated, but then he did what she asked.

Paige exhaled nervously, hoping her words came out the way she needed them to. "The truth is, Pierce, I've been attracted to you since the first day I met you, and now I'm in love with you."

Pierce raised his eyebrows, seemingly not comprehending.

"I am," she continued. "I've loved you for years, but after making love to you last night, well, now I don't ever want to be without you. Plus, baby, you can't deny there has always been a certain chemistry between us."

Pierce shook his head. "Please tell me you're kidding."

"Baby, I've never been more serious in my life."

He stared at her and then got up. "This is crazy."

"No, it's not. It's wonderful."

"*No*, Paige, it's horrible, because you and I can never be anything more than in-laws."

"Honey, please don't say that. Please just give what we have a chance, because deep down, I know you love me."

"No. I don't. I mean, I love you the way friends love each other, but that's where it ends."

"Like I said, you just need some time, and once you get used to the idea, you'll be fine."

"How on earth can you be in love with your sister's husband?"

"Because I just am. I love you, and I can't help it."

"Well, if that's really true, then now I'm even sorrier about sleeping with you."

"Please don't apologize, baby," she said, walking over and hugging him.

But Pierce pushed her away. "Paige, no. And I think it's time you got dressed."

"Pierce, please don't do this. Don't give up on our destiny."

"I need to take a shower and get ready, so I really need you to leave."

"But Pierce—"

"Paige, please go."

She gaped at him with sad eyes but quickly decided Pierce didn't mean any of what he was saying. He simply felt guilty about what he'd done to Camille—especially with him being the decent man he was—but by this evening, he'd feel a lot differently. He'd spend today reminiscing about the passionate love they'd made, and then he'd think about Camille and her affair with William. A thousand thoughts would circulate his mind, and in a few hours he'd realize Paige was right. He would know she'd been correct in her assessment of them and that he *was* in love with her, and that he wanted nothing else to do with his wife. By this evening, he'd be begging Paige to rock his world again— he would beg her to do so from now on.

Chapter 24

$\mathscr{I}$t was seven o'clock in the evening, and Paige had waited as long as she could. She'd waited all day, and it was time—that she headed up to Pierce's suite, that is. So she took a final look at her flawless makeup and loosely curled hair and then stepped out of the bathroom and stood in front of the full-length mirror. The bright fuchsia negligee fit perfectly and showed more cleavage than most women would want it to, and Paige knew she was ready.

She slipped on her all-weather coat, tied the belt, slipped into her black stilettos, picked up her wallet, and left her room. She couldn't wait to see Pierce again, now that he'd had ample time to reflect on the last twenty-four hours. She couldn't wait to hear how he now agreed that last night hadn't been a mistake at all, and instead had been a blessing for both of them.

Paige was so tickled, she could hardly make it to the elevator fast enough—but her spirit was broken when she saw Camille calling. "What do you want?" she yelled out loud, and the man and woman passing by looked as though they were afraid of her and like she was a nutcase.

"Hey?" Paige answered with no enthusiasm.

"Hey, how's it goin'? I hadn't heard from you yet today, so I figured I'd give you a call."

You haven't heard from me because I don't wanna talk to you. "I've been very busy with my client."

"That's what I kinda thought."

Then why are you calling me, Camille?

"Is everything okay?" Camille asked. "You seem quiet."

"I told you, I'm busy," Paige said loudly.

"Are you sure nothing's wrong? Because you don't sound right."

"I'm fine. My client had a lot of media interviews, more than I'd planned on, and I'm pretty exhausted."

"Well, it's not like I really wanted anything...well, actually there is one thing I wanted to share with you."

"What?"

"I've decided that I'm not going down without a fight."

"Meaning?"

"I'm not gonna sit back the way I have over the last few days, feeling defeated and hoping the truth comes out. What I'm gonna do is hire a better computer expert and do everything else I can to prove my innocence."

Paige didn't like what she was hearing but said, "Good for you."

"I won't lose Pierce over some crazy misunderstanding. I just won't."

"I don't blame you," Paige said, trying to sound supportive.

"Okay, then," Camille said. "I'd better let you get some rest."

"I'll try to call you tomorrow."

"I love you."

"Talk to you later," Paige said, ending the call and tossing her phone inside her coat pocket.

When she turned the corner, she walked halfway down the corridor and knocked on Pierce's door.

"Who is it?" he asked.

"Me."

"Paige?"

"Yes."

There was silence, but then Pierce let her in. "What is it that you want?"

"To talk to you."

"There's really nothing to say."

Paige closed the door behind her and took a seat on the brown velvet sectional in the living room area. Pierce leaned against the wall in front of her and next to the large television. "So, have you thought more about what I told you this morning?" she asked.

"As far as you and me?"

"Yes."

"If you want to know the truth, I've thought about nothing else."

Paige beamed with relief. "I knew you'd finally realize that our being together wasn't a mistake. You and I having business in the same city at the same time is no coincidence, Pierce. It was God's plan for us."

"Okay, let me stop you right there. God has absolutely nothing to do with the terrible thing you and I did. We both chose to have sex, and I selfishly chose to commit adultery on my wife. Period."

Paige couldn't believe he was still talking this way, and she was deeply tired of hearing about Camille. Poor, pitiful, pathetic Camille. That witch.

"Okay," she said. "I understand your remorse, but what matters now is that things are over between you and Camille, and I'm the one who genuinely loves you. I'm the one who will always be faithful to you and will take care of you no matter what. Your happiness is my only priority, and I'll do anything you want. I would even give my life for you, Pierce, if it became necessary."

Pierce seemed dumbfounded, but she knew it was because

no woman, not even Camille, had ever vowed to love him so intensely and devotedly. He was shocked to learn that after wasting fifteen long, miserable years with her, he'd finally found the woman of his dreams—the woman he'd fantasized about and secretly loved, even if he wouldn't admit it.

"Why are you looking at me so strangely?" she asked, smiling, when he still didn't speak.

"Because I'm trying my best to figure out where all this is coming from. I mean, Paige, it's as if I don't even know you anymore."

"This is who I've been all along, but until now I was never able to express how I feel about you."

"Then I really hate to hear that."

"Why?"

"Because the feeling isn't mutual. I'm in love with Camille, and that's never going to change."

Paige didn't understand him. "Not even after how stupid she made you look? You still love her even after she slept around on you behind your back and then lied about it?"

"She's my wife, and yes, I love her."

Paige heard him loudly and clearly and knew she had to do something. So she stood up, opened her coat, and let it drop to the ground.

"Paige, please," he said, but before he could get his words out, she was toe to toe with him, wrapping her arms around his shoulders and kissing him.

Pierce pushed her with much force, and she stumbled backward and onto the couch. "Baby, what's wrong with you?" she asked, trying to steady herself.

"Paige, I want you out of here."

"But baby, I don't understand. Sweetheart, Camille doesn't even want you. She was just saying today how glad she was that you'd moved out and how she couldn't wait to file for a divorce."

Sorrow filled Pierce's eyes, and Paige knew she'd finally gotten to him. He would never go begging and pleading back to Camille now.

"Did you hear me, baby?" she asked.

"Stop calling me that! Don't you ever call me that again. And for the record, I don't care what Camille told you. I love my wife, and I'm going to do whatever it takes to work things out with her. Now get out of here," he said, snatching her coat and forcing it into her chest.

Paige broke into tears. "So, you don't want me?"

"My God, woman, how many other ways do I need to say it?"

"Pierce, I'm begging you...please don't do this."

"I'm asking you nicely to please leave."

Paige rushed toward him, trying to clasp her arms around his neck, but this time Pierce snapped.

"Didn't I tell you to get out of here?" he shouted, grabbing her by the arm and dragging her toward the door.

"I just wanna be with you," she said, groveling. "That's all I've ever wanted. Can't you understand that?" Pierce opened the door and led her across the threshold, but she stepped back inside. "Can I at least get my wallet and put my coat on?"

Pierce stormed over to the sofa, grabbed the wallet, and gave it to her. Paige looked at him with pleading eyes but saw only fury in his. He seemed so perturbed and disgusted by her presence, and none of what was happening made sense. Had he used her and was now simply dismissing her? Had he slept with her and then dumped her like she was no one special? Like she wasn't good enough? Like she couldn't hold a candle to his precious Camille? Was he rejecting her and treating her just as coldly as her parents? Had Pierce been fooling her all these years—making her think they were soul mates and that they would one day be together? Could he really be that cruel, now knowing just how much she loved him? Would he really make hot, passionate love to her and then pretend it never happened?

Paige looked at Pierce, he glared back, and then he slammed the door in her face. Just like that, things were over between them, and he was planning to go back to Camille. He couldn't wait to let bygones be bygones and get back to his fairytale lifestyle. She could see it in his eyes and demeanor.

But Paige had news for him. Nothing in life was ever that easy, not for any of us—and she would prove it.

Chapter 25

*H*ours had passed, it was three in the morning, and Paige was a nervous wreck. After leaving Pierce's suite and coming straight back to hers, she'd paced back and forth, cried her eyes out, paced the floor again, and then ordered up a bottle of Riesling wine, which was all gone. Now she tossed and turned in bed, trying to get some sleep, and it was all because she couldn't stop thinking about Pierce and how she would make things right between them. She pondered, deliberated, and contemplated her next move, but just then it dawned on her what the real problem was—the reason Pierce was so confused about his feelings. It was Camille and the fact that she was still in the way of their happiness. If it wasn't for her, Pierce wouldn't feel so guilty, and he would be free to love Paige the way she needed him to. Of course, Paige didn't like how he'd willingly slept with her and then suddenly rejected her, but she understood why he had. He didn't want people to start talking, something that was bound to happen once a few gossipmongers learned he had left his wife for her sister.

Like with any other local scandal, yes, folks would whisper and criticize them, but it wouldn't be long before all conversations ceased. People would speak less and less about it, and in a few months they'd forget what had actually happened and would find someone else's business to stick their noses into.

Still, Paige knew none of that mattered to a man like Pierce, someone who would never want to bring even a few weeks of shame to his family and who would do whatever he had to in order to protect them. He would even sacrifice being with Paige, the new love of his life, just so he could do the right thing. What *he* thought was right, anyway.

Paige tossed and turned another three hours, but when she couldn't take it anymore, she reached over, turned on the light, picked up the cordless phone, and dialed Pierce's room. They would both be in Las Vegas another three days, so she had plenty of time to change his mind about them. She would get him to see that their being together was inevitable, and that there was no sense trying to fight it.

The phone rang until the hotel's voicemail system picked up. Paige listened but then hung up, wondering where Pierce could be when it was barely after six o'clock. Maybe he was already in the shower or had gone down for an early breakfast. She wasn't sure exactly, so she took a chance on dialing his cell phone. It rang three times before Pierce answered.

"What is it, Paige?" he said, sounding irritated.

"Um, I just wanted to talk to you for a few minutes if you don't mind."

"About what?"

"Last night."

"And?"

"Well, for one thing, I'm sorry I made you so upset."

"Look, I'm over all that, and I suggest you get over it, too," he said matter-of-factly.

"It's not that easy," she said. "But maybe if we could have lunch or dinner and talk about this face-to-face, I could explain things better to you."

"Nope. Not gonna happen."

"But why?"

"For one thing, I don't want to, and for another, I'm already pulling up to the airport," he said and then told what must have been his driver, "Yes, I'm flying out on American, so right here is good."

"You're leaving?" she said, trying to calm herself.

"Yep. Called and changed my reservation as soon as you left last night."

"But I thought your conference didn't end until Friday."

"Yeah, well, thanks to you, it ended a lot sooner. For me, anyway, but actually I'm glad, because I need to get home to Camille and my children. I need to spend every day I can making things up to them."

Paige's moment of sadness turned ugly. "So what you're saying is that you got what you wanted from me and now you're rushing home to your wife?"

"Thank you so much," he told his driver.

"Did you hear me, Pierce?"

"Look," he said. "Two nights ago was the biggest mistake of my life, but it's over."

"I can't believe you."

"Believe what? That I love my wife and not you?"

"But that's just it, Pierce, you do love me. You love everything about me, and the only reason you're acting like this is because you feel obligated to Camille."

"Of course I feel obligated to her. She's been my wife for fifteen years, and I'm still in love with her. But even if I wasn't, I could never love you."

"What?"

"It's just a fact, Paige. You're a nice enough woman...or at least I thought you were before this week, but I'm not attracted to you in that way."

"Oh really? Then why did you tell me the other night that you've always thought I was beautiful?"

"Because you are. But that was just a compliment."

Paige's face softened, the rage in her dissipated, tears seeped from her eyes. "Gosh, Pierce, are you that naïve? Have you forgotten that Camille wants nothing to do with you?"

"That's not true."

"Of course it is."

"No it's not. After I hung up with the airline, she and I talked for more than three hours, and we're going to be fine."

Paige's stomach churned. "So that's it? You're ending things with me because of her?"

"You and I had sex, Paige. One time, and that was it."

"No, we had an affair, you fell in love with me, and now you're trying to cut me off."

Pierce laughed. "You must be out of your mind."

"No, I'm the same person you manipulated, brought back to your hotel suite, and then took advantage of."

"You know what? I'm done with this conversation," he said.

"Pierce? Pierce? Hello?"

He hadn't even allowed Paige to respond. Still, she sat there, holding the phone to her ear, barely able to move. He truly didn't want her, and it was all because of Camille and a few lame words she'd obviously said to him during some three-hour chat Paige hadn't counted on.

But Paige wasn't worried about it, because once Pierce saw Camille face-to-face, he'd be reminded of her infidelity, and he would go back to hating her again. He would then call Paige, apologizing and telling her how much he loved her and missed her, and he would then be on his way over to her place. He would realize who loved him most and who he could ultimately be the happiest with, and all this madness about his getting back together with Camille would be over. He would end things with his wife for good this time, and Paige now felt a lot better. She could see things much more clearly and was comforted.

She was relieved and finally drifted off to sleep.

Chapter 26

*I*t was noon on Saturday, and Paige had been home for three days now. She'd planned on staying in Vegas until Friday, but seeing as Pierce had left so abruptly on Wednesday morning, she'd changed her ticket and flown out that evening herself. She'd wanted to stay longer, but since she'd been there all alone, she hadn't seen a reason for it. The only problem was, she hadn't heard a peep from Pierce yet, or from Camille for that matter, and she was starting to get worried. She'd even gone as far as calling his office yesterday, but to her surprise, his executive assistant had told her he wouldn't be in until Monday. Paige had just assumed that since he'd left the conference early, he'd go back to work business as usual. But he hadn't, and that could only mean one thing. He was spending as much time as he could with that sister of hers and maybe the idea that Camille had messed around on him no longer mattered. Paige had been sure that once he saw Camille again, he wouldn't be able to get past what she'd done to him, but apparently he had, and they were working things out the way Pierce had anticipated.

But Paige wondered how great things would continue being for them if Camille were to find out about Vegas and what had evolved between her husband and sister. She wondered just how smoothly things would continue then.

She pulled out a photo album, opened it, and ran her hand slowly across one of Camille and Pierce's wedding photos. She did the same with a photo of Camille and Pierce that had been taken one year at their parents' during Christmas dinner, and with a professional family photo of Pierce, Camille, PJ, and Crystal, and she also admired at least thirty other pictures Camille had given her over the years. They were all unique in one way or another, but they did have one thing in common: Camille's face was completely blacked out on all of them. It was as if she no longer existed, and Paige wished this was actually the case. She wished she could erase Camille from all their lives, so that she would never have to think about her again. She wanted Camille gone, and if she didn't hear from Pierce soon, she'd have to figure out how to make that happen. She didn't want to harm her sister physically, not if she didn't have to, but she wanted her to leave Pierce alone and find herself a new husband. That was all. And Paige didn't see where that was asking for too much.

She flipped through the album a second time but closed it when her phone rang. She rolled her eyes when Owen's number displayed.

"What?" she said, answering.

"Now, is that any way to greet the man who has the goods on you?"

"You've got nothing," she said.

"I know about that photo," he sang.

"My sister will never believe you."

"But it'll get her thinking and wondering why I would tell her something like that if it isn't true. Especially since I don't have a thing to gain from lying."

"She'll just think you're some disgruntled ex-boyfriend of mine who's looking to get back at me."

"Maybe. But I wonder how Pierce will feel about it. You know, he and I always clicked pretty well whenever you and I got to-gether with them."

Paige smiled at that one, because even if Pierce did believe Owen, she knew Pierce would never pursue it or mention any-thing to Camille, not when he and Paige had slept together. He wouldn't want to bring up anything that might lead Camille to think anything about him and her sister. Still, Paige didn't want Owen telling anyone anything and said, "How much do I owe you?"

"At least seven thousand. Maybe more. But seven will certainly make me forget I ever saw that picture of yours."

Paige hated this and regretted ever dating Owen. Worse, he didn't even have tangible proof, yet he was demanding the kind of money she didn't have. At the most, she had fifteen hundred dollars in a money market account and maybe another two thou-sand dollars she could scrape together through credit card cash advances, but that was it.

"So, can I pick up my hush money this afternoon?" he asked, once he realized she hadn't responded.

"All I have right now is thirty-five hundred, so you'll have to wait another month or so for the other half."

"Not good enough."

"What do you mean?"

"I want it all."

"But I don't have it, Owen."

"Then you leave me no choice."

"Why are you doing this?"

"Because you're no good, Paige. You used me, and when you were finished you tossed me aside like some stray animal. And I'm not letting you get away with it. So, again, I want my seven thou-sand dollars or else."

"Owen, I'm really sorry for the way I treated you, and you're right," she said, trying a different approach. "I never should have taken advantage of your generosity, and I was very wrong for that. But right now I don't have the total amount you're asking for."

"That's really too bad. But for the last time, I want all or nothing."

Paige didn't know what else to say, and since she couldn't magically produce thousands of dollars, she would just have to deal with the consequences. It would be his word against hers, anyway, so how much damage could he really do?

"I'm sorry you feel the need to blackmail me, but hey, you do what you have to do. Although I must say, Owen, I really thought you were better than this. I thought you were a good man."

"See, but that's just it. I am a good man. A good man who's tired of women like you who think they can treat people any way they want and then move on to their next victim. This isn't the first time a woman has done this kind of thing to me, but with you, I finally decided to do something about it."

"Like I said, I'm really sorry."

"I'm sure you are, but as my friends and I used to say when we were kids, 'Sorry didn't do it, you did.'"

Paige closed her eyes, praying Owen was only bluffing, but somehow she knew he wasn't. She could tell he was dead serious and realized maybe this new idea that had just popped into her head might buy her some time.

"Can you give me until the middle of next week?"

"Why?"

"I'm going to apply for a bank loan."

"From who?" Owen said, cracking up. "Your brother-in-law?"

"No, but can you wait just a few more days?"

"I'll think about it."

"I hope you will."

"Okay, fine. I'll give you until Wednesday and not a day longer."

Paige breathed easier and hoped that when Wednesday arrived she'd have figured out another way to secure even more time, since there was no way anyone, not even Pierce, would give her a no-collateral personal loan. Her credit was shot, and it wouldn't even behoove her to fill out an application, let alone expect anyone to approve it. So the best she could do was hold Owen off for as long as possible, or at least until her relationship with Pierce was solid. She would say or do whatever she had to for the time being, because she didn't have a choice.

Chapter 27

With the exception of a few minutes here and there, Paige literally hadn't slept a wink. Not last night or the night before, and she was deliriously exhausted. She also hadn't eaten in three whole days, had only spoken to Karla for a few minutes on Saturday—claiming she had an extremely busy weekend schedule and would call her early this week—and the only reason she'd forced herself to drink water was because she didn't want to become dehydrated. She'd read a long time ago that the human body could survive for a while without food but not much more than three days without water, and for some reason she'd never forgotten that.

Today, though, it was early Monday morning, and she couldn't dial Pierce's work number fast enough.

"Pierce Montgomery's office," his assistant said. "Eleanor speaking."

"Hi Eleanor. Is he in?"

"Sure, may I tell him who's calling?"

"Yes, please let him know it's his sister-in-law."

"No problem."

Paige waited a few seconds, and then Eleanor said, "I'll put you right through."

"Thank you," she said, and there was a short silence.

"This is Pierce speaking."

"Hey, how are you?" she asked.

"I'm good. You?"

"Not so well."

Pierce said nothing else, and it sounded as though he was handling papers in the background.

"Look, Pierce. It's been five days since we last talked, so why haven't you called me?"

"There was no reason to."

"Not even after we shared such a special time together? Not even after I poured my heart out to you the way I did?"

"Paige, you're really trying my patience, but I'm going to explain this to you once and for all. What happened in Vegas will always stay in Vegas because it never should have happened in the first place. You and I did a terrible thing, but we have to go on with our lives. You with whomever and me with my wife."

Paige's heart pounded against her chest. "Pierce, please don't cut me off like this. Please don't stay with Camille when you know she can't be trusted. She's only going to hurt you again and again and again."

"She and I have hurt each other. But that's all in the past."

Paige heard her call waiting signal, looked at the screen, and saw that it was Camille. She wanted to kill that heifer. Her sister was still coming out on top and getting everything she wanted, and Paige hated her for it.

"How can you pretend that Camille hasn't done anything, Pierce?" she asked, ignoring the incoming call. "How could you forgive her?"

"Because she's my wife, and I love her. But that's all beside the point, Paige, and the bottom line is this: I don't owe you or anyone else any explanations when it comes to my marriage."

"Pierce, please listen to me."

"No, I've heard more than enough from you, and after today, I don't want you calling my office or cell numbers again."

Paige's eyes filled with water and soon massive tears slid down her face.

"Did you hear me, Paige?" he asked sternly.

"Pierce . . . I'll . . . do . . . anything . . . but . . . please . . . don't . . . end . . . things . . . between . . . us. Baby, I love you so much, and you're all I have."

"Goodbye, Paige."

"But—" she tried saying. However, he was already gone and Paige was devastated.

She'd thought for sure that once he heard her voice, he would think about their intimate rendezvous at The Palazzo and would want to see her again. But for the first time since he'd initially begun trying to tell her he loved Camille and not her, she believed him. When he'd said their being together had been a mistake, she now knew he meant it. Worse, only minutes ago when he'd told her he didn't want her calling him again, she'd known he was serious. But none of what was happening made any sense, and she wondered why God was punishing her—why He was making things so incredibly hard for her when it came to getting what she wanted. Why was He allowing Camille to triumph yet again? Why would He do this after all the years Camille had been blessed with everything, while Paige continued having nothing and no one to love her?

It was times such as these when Paige wondered if life was actually worth living and whether it would be easier to simply give up. But the only thing was, there was way too much passion in her to do something like that. Right now, she was extremely depressed, but she would never surrender to Camille. She would never allow her to keep Pierce without a fight. There was no denying that Pierce wholeheartedly thought Camille was the best woman for him, but just as soon as Paige pulled herself together and plotted a better plan to break them up, Pierce would turn to her again. He would come to her and promise to never leave her from then on. He would thank her for hanging in there for as long as she had and would shower her with all the gifts she could imagine. Instead of Camille, she would be the one who finally had everything.

Pierce would commit his life to Paige until death, and there wouldn't be a single thing anyone could do about it.

Chapter 28

$\mathcal{O}$nly two days had passed since Pierce had told her not to call him again, but Paige had already come up with a brilliant new scheme.

"I'm so glad we were able to get out and do some shopping," Paige said as Camille steered her SUV away from the mall and down the highway.

"Me too. We've both been through so much, and I'm glad things are finally getting back to normal."

"I know. And Camille, I have to tell you, I couldn't be happier about you and Pierce reconciling and fixing things between you."

"Thank you for saying that, because it was certainly a close call. There were days when I thought our marriage was over for good."

"I did, too, but now everything is fine, and we can thank God for the outcome."

"Isn't that the truth? But there is one thing that still bothers me," Camille said.

"What's that?"

"Those doggoned email messages. I mean, no matter how hard we try to figure out who sent them, we still haven't been success-ful."

"It's definitely very odd, but if I were you, I wouldn't worry about it. You and Pierce are happy again, and that's all that matters. And hey, don't forget to stop by the coffee shop so I can run in and get us a couple of Frappuccinos," Paige said.

"Oh yeah, that's right. Actually, I think the nearest one is just down the road."

"Sounds good. I love, love, love those," Paige said, and got a kick out of how naïve Camille was. The woman was having what she thought was the time of her life with her baby sister and had no idea Paige had slept with her husband just one week ago. She also had no clue that things were about to get worse.

They drove another mile or two, turned into the parking lot of a locally owned coffee establishment, and Camille's cell rang. She pulled it out of her handbag, smiled at whomever was calling, and said, "Hey sweetheart."

Paige knew immediately it was Pierce and wanted to snatch that phone out of her hand. Nonetheless, she smiled, too, pretending she was overjoyed.

"We're getting some drinks, and then once I drop Paige off, I'll be home," Camille told him. Then she paused, obviously listening to what Pierce said next. "This sounds serious," she commented, and then there was more silence. "I promise I'll be there within the hour...I love you, too, baby."

Camille set her phone down, and Paige said, "Wow. Sounds like somebody misses their wife and wants her home."

"Yeah, but it sounds like something's wrong."

"What do you mean?"

"I don't know. All he said was that it was important and that he needed to speak to me face-to-face."

Paige panicked, wondering if he was going to come clean about Vegas. If he was, she knew she had to get inside the coffee shop now. "Okay, so what kind of frappe do you want?"

"Mmm...I guess I'll have my usual, mocha."

"I think I will, too," Paige said, opening the door and stepping out of the vehicle. "I'll be back."

Paige strolled inside, ordered two mocha Frappuccinos, paid the young blond, waited a few minutes, and then picked up their drinks from the other end of the counter. She moved farther around the corner, pretending to get napkins and straws, but quickly pulled three white pills from her purse and dropped them into one of the cups. She scanned the area, making sure no one had seen her, and went back out to the SUV. When she got in, she passed the tainted drink to Camille, and Camille took two long sips. Paige did the same, and Camille drove off. But as soon as they did, Paige set her drink into the cup holder.

"Hey sis," she said. "I just thought about something. Do you mind stopping at Wal-Mart, so I can pick up some printer paper?"

"Of course. If you want, we can drive to one of the office stores."

"No, that's sort of out of the way, so Wal-Mart will be fine. Plus, I only need a small package to tide me over and then I can just get my regular supply from Office Depot later this week."

When they arrived at the store ten minutes later, Camille pulled into a parking stall and leaned her head back.

"Are you okay?" Paige asked, smirking.

"I don't know. For some reason, I feel dizzy and like I can barely keep my eyes open."

"Really? Well, maybe I should drive," Paige said, realizing those sleeping pills she'd drugged Camille with were quickly taking effect.

"Maybe you should," she said, and Paige got out, went around to the driver's side, helped her sister onto the pavement, and then led her around to the passenger seat. She helped her get comfortable, buckled her seatbelt, and then rushed back to the driver's side and took off. Camille was fast asleep, and Paige sped toward their next destination and made a phone call. When the man answered, she looked over at her sister and said, "She's out cold. See you in twenty minutes."

Chapter 29

Paige drove across the gravel parking lot and stopped in front of the room she'd reserved early yesterday. This wasn't the best motel she'd ever seen, and it certainly wasn't located on the best side of town, but it was perfect for what she was conspiring. For two full days and two full nights, she'd seriously considered a few different ideas, so that she wouldn't have to go this far, but she hadn't seen where she had any other choice—not when she'd already endured a full-fledged beating from Derrick and then deceived Covington Park Police Department personnel regarding her rape. She'd gone to what she thought was the extreme, but it still hadn't worked. She'd even caused a temporary separation between Camille and Pierce, flown nearly two thousand miles across the country, and slept with him, but her sister and brother-in-law had found their way back to each other like nothing had happened. So on this occasion, Paige decided it was time she gave Pierce the proof he needed, the kind he could see with his own eyes.

Paige stepped outside of the vehicle, closed the door, and walked around to where Camille was sitting.

"Hey sis," she said, shaking her. "Wake up."

But Camille didn't move.

Now Paige wished she'd only given her two pills instead of three, because she seemed nearly unconscious. She shook her again with all her might, and when Camille moaned and slightly moved her head and body, Paige beckoned for the tall man to come and help her. Thankfully, it was dark outside and the room was on the far end toward the back, because she would never want anyone to see what she and her new friend, Leonard, were up to. That was the man's name—the homeless man she'd found wandering about yesterday when she'd driven out here to case the place. He'd looked like a natural bum and like he hadn't bathed in months, but Paige had struck up a conversation with him and asked if he wanted to make a hundred dollars. He'd hurried and said yes, so Paige had rented the room they were now escorting Camille into, so she could help clean him up. Then, when Paige had returned from the nearest Target, purchasing several kinds of toiletries, he'd showered, shaved, and eaten the food she'd brought him. Shortly after that, she'd run to Macy's and charged a pair of black dress pants, a white- and black-striped button-down shirt, and a package of Jockey underwear on her credit card. It had all been worth it, too, because the new Leonard looked like a million bucks and very much like the kind of man Camille would consort with—he looked like William, the fictitious man Pierce thought she'd had an affair with.

"Help me get her into bed," Paige told him, and they gently laid her on her back. The print bedspread was already turned down, so Paige removed Camille's shoes and jeans and pulled her thick off-white V-neck sweater over her head.

"Where am I?" she asked in a groggy tone.

"You're home, sweetie," Paige said.

"I'm...so...tired," she said, dozing off again.

"So, who exactly is this nice lady?" Leonard wanted to know.

"No one important," Paige said.

"Well, you must *really* hate her."

"It's a long story."

"Okay, just so I'm sure," he said, changing the subject. "All I have to do is sit here and wait for her husband to show up and then say, 'I'm William'?"

"Yep."

"And then what?"

"Well, for one thing, her husband will be pretty upset to find her at a motel with another man, so that's when you'll tell him you're sorry and that you think it's best for you to leave. Oh, and when you let him in, I want you to have your shirt open."

Leonard unbuttoned it right then. "This man isn't going to be so angry that he'll want to tear my head off, will he?"

"It's possible, but all you have to do is run, and I'll be waiting down the street for you."

"Whoaaa, now wait. If I'm gonna have to get my tail kicked, then that's gonna cost you another hundred."

"Excuse me?"

"Another hundred or I walk."

Paige laughed and grabbed her purse. "You drive a hard bargain, Leonard."

"Hey, I just wanna be paid."

"I hear you."

Camille moved her head to the side and slightly turned her body but never woke up.

"Okay," Paige said. "I'm out of here."

"How long do you think it'll be?"

"Less than an hour."

"Also," Leonard said when she opened the door, "what's your name?"

"Trish."

"Oh. Well, nice doin' business with you, Trish."

"Same here, and I'll see you in a little while."

Paige walked a quarter of a mile from the motel, got into a rental car, and dialed Pierce. He answered in a huff.

"Paige, didn't I ask you not to call me anymore?"

"I know, but this is important, and it'll only take a few minutes."

"What?" he yelled.

"It's Camille."

"What about Camille?"

"When she dropped me off at home, she went to meet that William guy."

"Oh, Paige, please stop it."

"I'm telling you the truth. I knew the only way you'd believe me was if I had proof, so I hired a private investigator to follow her. And he just called me."

"I just spoke with Camille a little over an hour ago, so you're lying."

"Then why isn't she home yet?"

"I don't know."

"Well, I do. She's at a motel," Paige said and gave him the address and room number.

"You'd better not be lying to me."

"I'm not, and I'm only doing this because I love you, Pierce. I told you I would do anything for you, and I meant it."

"Yeah, whatever," he said.

Paige knew he'd hung up on her, but this time she didn't care, because once he saw his perfect little wife shacked up in some shabby motel room with her lover, he'd practically come crawling to Paige, thanking her and begging her to forgive him. Camille was finally getting what she deserved, and Paige wanted to get out of the car and scream to the heavens—she wanted to thank God for all that was happening. He'd taken an excessively long time answering her prayers, but what mattered was that He had in fact come through for her. He'd finally given her what she'd asked for, and she was satisfied.

Chapter 30

As promised, Paige had waited for Leonard, and thankfully, all Pierce had done was punch him one good time and tell him to get out. Of course, Leonard hadn't been happy about it, but when Paige had offered him another fifty dollars, he'd seemed content. She'd then asked him where he wanted to go, and he'd told her to drop him off at a well-known shelter. Paige had thanked him for all his help, and he'd wished her well. Now she was standing in front of the overnight box at the car rental company, preparing to deposit the key to the vehicle she'd rented. When she did, she walked over and sat inside Derrick's brand-new two-seater, and he pulled off.

"I don't have the slightest idea what you're up to, but I've got some bad news," he said.

"What?"

"You know that day I called you? While you were at O'Hare, getting ready to fly to Vegas?"

"Yeah, what about it?"

"Well, Andrea heard everything I said to you."

Paige bugged her eyes. "She what? How?"

Derrick sighed and wouldn't look at her. "Paige, I'm so sorry."

"How did this happen, Derrick?" she ranted.

"Before I called you on my office phone, she'd called me on my cell, but I guess I didn't end my call with her. I must've just set it on my desk, thinking she'd hung up."

"Please tell me you're joking."

"I'm not...and she heard everything. About the rape we faked and how you're trying to take your sister's husband from her."

"Oh my God," Paige said, dropping her face into her hands.

"I messed up, Paige, and that's not the worst of it."

"Meaning?"

"She also heard me say how you've let me bring my women over to your condo, so she's threatening to tell Camille as payback."

"She doesn't even know my sister, does she?"

"They go to the same hair salon, remember?"

This was bad. Especially since Andrea had never cared all that much for Paige.

"You have to stop her, Derrick."

"How? Andrea is mad as hell, and she's only two seconds from kicking me out of my own house and divorcing me. So there's no reasoning with her."

"How could you be so careless?" Paige demanded to know.

"I'm sorry."

If he said he was sorry one more time, Paige wasn't sure what she might do to him. "Do you realize what this might mean?"

Derrick drove through an intersection but didn't respond.

"Do you? It'll mean all my hard work was for nothing. If Andrea tells Camille anything, Pierce will never speak to me again. He'll hate me from now on."

"I wish there was something I could do."

Paige wanted to slap Derrick silly, but she couldn't focus on him right now. What she had to do was direct her attention toward the matter at hand—this disaster Derrick had so recklessly created and the nightmare that might result from it.

For the next twenty minutes of the drive to her home, they rode in total silence. No radio, CD, or anything. So she sort of jumped when her phone rang. She checked the screen and was surprised Owen hadn't called her first thing this morning since it was Wednesday.

"Yes," she said.

"Hey, I just called to tell you, I'm through."

"I'm not sure I understand."

"You're free and clear."

Paige was shocked. "You mean that?"

"Yep. You no longer owe me a single dime, and this is the last time you'll hear from me."

"Why'd you change your mind? Of course, I'm very grateful, but I just wondered."

"You're not worth it, Paige. You're just not worth the trouble."

Paige was speechless and, strangely enough, hurt.

"You have a nice life," he said, and Paige was glad this whole blackmail drama was over with.

"Who was that?" Derrick asked.

"Owen."

"What did he want?"

"Nothing."

"You know, while you were on the phone, something dawned on me," he said. "Maybe you should tell your sister everything yourself."

"Are you crazy?"

"I'm just trying to figure out how you can fix this."

"Derrick, just shut up, okay?"

"Fine."

Paige never said another word to him for the rest of the ride. Instead, she hoped and prayed Andrea wouldn't tell. She prayed for a complete miracle.

Chapter 31

$\mathcal{P}$aige glanced at the clock for what seemed like the millionth time, wishing Pierce would call her. It was three in the afternoon, he wasn't at work, and his cell had continually gone to voicemail. Had he and Camille somehow worked things out again? They couldn't have. Not after last night. Not when Pierce had gone to that motel and witnessed everything. He'd caught her with another man, for God's sake, and she couldn't imagine any husband forgiving his wife for something so callous. Would he?

Paige took a drag of her cigarette, a habit she'd picked up only a couple of hours ago right after returning from the gas station, and wondered what she should do. Maybe she should try Pierce's cell phone again, especially since she hadn't done so for at least five minutes. Or maybe she should try calling Andrea. This morning she'd called Derrick, checking to see if he'd been able to talk some sense into her, but he hadn't. He'd told her how Andrea was no longer speaking to him, and that she had indeed decided to divorce him. Last night, Derrick had said she'd only threatened him with divorce, but apparently things had changed rather quickly.

Paige picked up her home phone, preparing to call Derrick so she could ask him for Andrea's number, but she set it back on its base when her cell rang. "Finally," she said, rushing out of the kitchen and into the living room to get it.

"Hey," she said but realized she'd answered way too quickly since it wasn't Pierce at all. It was Camille.

"Hey sis," Camille said, sounding wounded and troubled. "Girl, you won't believe what happened."

"What?"

"Pierce found me at a motel with some man who claimed he was that William guy. The man who I've supposedly been having an affair with."

"No way."

"Yes, and Pierce is angry enough to kill someone. We argued until the wee hours of the morning, and then when the kids went to school, he packed his things and left. And Paige, I think he's gone for good this time," she said, crying. "He was so hurt and disappointed."

"But how did you end up at a hotel?"

"I don't know. The last thing I remember is you and I stopping for coffee."

"Well, that's strange, because right after that, you drove me home."

"All I know is that Pierce found me half-naked, and I can't explain why."

"Do you think maybe you're having memory problems?" Paige said, lighting another cigarette and feeling a hundred percent better about things.

"Funny you would say that, because I'm starting to think the same thing. There has to be something wrong, otherwise how could I have sent emails to someone I don't know, end up in bed with him, and then not remember any of it?"

"I think you need to see a doctor."

"Paige, I really need you right now. I feel like I'm losing my mind, and I don't know if I can handle this."

"Do you want me to come over?"

"Can you? I'm going to call Mom and Dad, too, because it's time I tell them what's going on, but I really need my sister."

"I'll be there soon," Paige said.

She went into her bedroom, dropped her phone inside her tote, grabbed her leather jacket, and hurried out to her car. She couldn't have been more thrilled. Her plan had worked perfectly, and now that even Camille knew Pierce wasn't coming back to her, Paige couldn't stop smiling. She actually laughed out loud as she drove out of her subdivision, heading to her sister's house—the house she would soon be living in and completely taking over. This had all been a long time coming, but now that the day was here, she decided it had all been well worth waiting for. It was true that she'd had to stoop to the lowest of levels and create more trickery and deception than most people saw in movies, but this was the reason she'd won. Her willingness to do whatever it took to get what she wanted had paid off, and if more people shared her philosophy they'd get what they wanted, too. But maybe they didn't have the kind of drive or desire she had and would simply have to settle on being miserable and unsatisfied for the rest of their lives. If so, she felt sorry for them and wished them well.

Chapter 32

As soon as Paige got out of her car and walked up to the front door, she rang the doorbell and looked around at all the beautiful leaves that had fallen onto the ground. She wasn't sure why Pierce hadn't called the lawn service to remove them, and she would have to make sure to remind him about it. There was so much involved and so much that had to be done when one lived in a huge house, and she would certainly do a much better job of keeping things in order around here than her sister had. She would be a better wife, a better lover, and even a better mother to her niece and nephew. She would show everyone that Paige Donahue —Paige Donahue Montgomery—had arrived.

Camille opened the door, but interestingly enough, all she did was stare at Paige and walk away. So Paige walked inside, closed the door, and followed her into the kitchen. Camille stood with her arms folded, and Paige sat at the island.

"You know, I've thought about this for hours now," Camille said. "And all I wanna know is, why?"

Paige didn't like the look on her sister's face or the eerie vibe overtaking the room. "Why what?"

"Why do you hate me so much? Why would you go out of your way to destroy me like this?"

Paige could barely breathe. "I don't know what you're talking about."

"Of course you do. And to think I brought you into my home and trusted you."

"Look," Paige said, not knowing where this was going or what Camille had discovered. "I don't have the slightest idea what you mean."

"I mean how you moved in here all innocently and then sent those email messages from my computer."

"What?" Paige yelled, acting as though she didn't have a clue.

"Yes, you sent the emails, Paige, so don't lie. And the sad part of all is that had my sweet little Crystal not overheard me early this morning talking to Mom about those messages and who could have possibly used my computer, I still wouldn't know it was you."

"You're crazy. And why in the world would you bring an innocent child into this?"

"Because she saw you, Paige. She saw you tiptoeing out of my office one night when you were staying here, and she said you had papers in your hand."

"That's not true."

"It is. And even when I wondered if maybe she'd made a mistake, my hesitation was put completely to rest when your friend's wife called me."

Paige's body fell limp.

"Yeah, that's right," Camille said. "Andrea called me right before noon and told me how you were never raped and that you've been after Pierce for a long time now."

"Andrea? Who's Andrea?"

"Don't play dumb with me, Paige. You know exactly who I'm talking about and that she's telling the truth."

Paige stood up in a huff. "This is crazy, and I'm not about to waste any more time listening to this foolishness. You're just mad because your perfect little life is falling apart and you need someone to blame."

Camille shook her head, but when the doorbell rang, she left the room. Paige didn't like what was happening and knew she had to get out of there. Although, actually, not all was lost, because even though Camille was on to some of what she'd done, she still couldn't prove a single thing. So all Paige had to do was find Pierce. She needed to see him, because no matter how much Camille thought she had figured out, there was no fixing her marriage, not when Pierce had caught her with her lover.

Paige grabbed her tote but stopped in her tracks when her mother and father entered the room.

"You disgust me," Maxine spat. "I knew you were up to something, and that's why I never wanted you moving in here. I knew it was a bad idea from the start."

"I'm outta here," Paige said.

"No, you're not going anywhere," Maxine said, standing in front of her, but Paige shoved her mother against the doorway.

"Oh my God, Mom," Camille said. "Are you okay?"

George helped Maxine recover her balance.

"Baby, I'm fine," Maxine said. "But this witch here," she said, pointing at Paige, "she's the one you need to worry about. She's the tramp who's obsessed with your husband, and she's dangerous. Not to mention she's the reason you ended up at that hotel last night."

"I know," Camille said.

Paige squinted her eyes at her sister. "What do you mean, *you know?*"

"Like she said," Pierce declared out of nowhere. "She knows you're the one who set her up. We all know."

Paige's body went into shock when she saw Leonard walking behind Pierce with his head down.

"Remember him?" Pierce said. "Remember the man you hired to ruin your sister?"

"You raggedy bastard," Paige said, charging toward Leonard and slamming both her fists against his chest repeatedly.

Pierce pulled her away from him. "Stop it, Paige!"

"I'm sorry," Leonard said. "But I just couldn't do it. I couldn't hurt these nice people the way you asked me to. So when Mr. Montgomery showed up at the hotel, I told him everything. I told him that I didn't think your name was really Trish, because I heard you tell someone on the phone your name was Paige. I heard you when I was in the bathroom."

"He's lying," Paige insisted. "He's just some dirty old homeless man who can barely even think straight."

"No, you're the one who's lying," Camille said. "You've hated me all these years, and that's the reason you did this. But I ask you again, why?"

Paige tossed Camille a dirty look. "Because you have everything. Even when we were kids, Mom and Dad always treated you better, and I've had to walk in your perfect little shadow since I was a toddler."

Camille shook her head. "That's not true, and you know it."

"It is true," Maxine said.

"Sweetheart, please don't," George told his wife.

"No, I'm sick of Paige, and it's time she knew the truth. Since the day you were born, I've never been able to stand you. And the only reason I kept you was because I didn't think I could live with the guilt of giving away my own child. But after this...after all the heartache and pain you've caused my sweet Camille, I wish I had. I wish I'd dumped you at the nearest orphanage or gave you to the family of that maniac who raped me."

Paige gazed at her mother and then looked at her father, Camille, Pierce, and Leonard. There was no way she'd heard her mother correctly.

"You look just like him," Maxine continued. "You're his spitting image, and now you're going to prison just like he did. And if we're lucky, you'll end up dying there, too—just like he did."

Paige burst into tears. "So, you're not my dad?" she said to George.

"No," he said. "I'm not. But I've always loved you like I was."

"And you?" she said to Camille. "You knew about this all along, didn't you? You knew my father was a rapist and you never told me?"

"No, Paige, I didn't. I had no idea."

"Yeah, right. And I'm supposed to believe that?"

"Well, I didn't, and no matter what you think, I've always loved you. I've always been there for you."

"Some good it did," Maxine said. "And—"

"That's enough," George exclaimed, interrupting her, and Maxine looked at him like he was crazy, the same as she'd been doing for years whenever he tried speaking up. Strange how it wasn't until now, at this very moment, that Paige realized her father hadn't treated her badly at all. Only her mother.

Still, tears soaked Paige's face, and when the doorbell rang, she stormed past Camille and through the family room. When she opened the door, however, she dropped her handbag and stumbled backward. Detectives Johnson and Anderson, the two detectives assigned to her rape case, stood in front of her.

Paige felt lightheaded and looked on in a daze.

Detective Anderson stepped inside and pulled out a pair of handcuffs. "Paige Donahue, you have the right to remain silent. Anything you say can and will be used against you in a court of law. You have the right to speak to an attorney. If you cannot afford an attorney, one will be provided for you. Do you understand these rights as they have been read to you?"

Paige heard every word he said but couldn't speak, not even if she wanted to. There was something she couldn't stop thinking about, though: she'd staged a phony rape and now learned she was the product of a real one.

The irony of it all was terrifying.

Epilogue

A Year Later

What a difference a year could make. Only twelve months ago, Paige had learned that the man she'd known as her father wasn't her father, and that her mother had hidden the truth from her for years. She'd also been completely exposed when it came to all the lying, plotting, and manipulating she'd done with her sister. They'd stopped her cold, and while Camille hadn't mentioned it that day Paige was arrested, Paige had discovered later on that Owen had in fact gotten his revenge. He had called Camille, after all, and told her about that photo he'd seen. Then there was Crystal, Paige's sweet little niece, who had seen her favorite auntie sneaking out of her mom's office. Paige, of course, hadn't counted on that particular scenario, but she hadn't blamed Crystal for telling. She also no longer blamed Andrea for calling Camille and divulging what she'd overheard either, especially since Paige knew she'd been wrong for offering Derrick a place to bring his women. She hadn't seen a problem with doing so back when it was happening, but today she was very sorry. She also regretted the way she'd convinced Derrick to help trigger an unnecessary crime investigation, and she was glad he hadn't had to do any jail time.

Nonetheless, however, the incident that had caught Paige totally off guard was when Leonard had showed up at her sister's.

She'd been stunned like no other time she could remember, and she hadn't been able to believe Leonard—poor, pitiable, homeless Leonard—had found the nerve to double-cross her. He'd truly gotten the best of her, because when he'd left the motel and gotten into the rental car with her, claiming Pierce had punched him and made him leave, she'd never questioned his honesty. She hadn't expected a man like Leonard to betray her, and she was shocked to know he hadn't even done it for more money. What she'd figured was that Pierce had probably paid him double the amount she'd given him, but as it had turned out, Leonard had only done what he thought was right. He was a genuinely good man who'd lost his job, wife, and children a few years back and had ended up on the streets. He was also very well-educated and now employed as an accountant at the same bank Pierce worked at. All he'd needed was a chance, Paige guessed, and interestingly enough, he'd written her a couple of letters, thanking her for picking him up and buying him clothes that day. He'd contacted her maybe a couple of months after she'd been admitted to the sanitarium, and she'd truly appreciated hearing from him.

Today, though, she was finally being released and going home with her best friend. She couldn't wait to start her new life and would forever be grateful to Karla for the loving way she'd stood by her. It was true that Paige's mental illness and all the dreadful things she'd done as a result of it had totally blindsided Karla, but Karla still hadn't turned her back on her—not even when it had taken Paige a full three months to accept and admit she was sick. Karla had never judged Paige, and she'd also done everything she could, trying to make things right between Paige and her family —something she was discussing right now with her therapist.

"Well, I must say," Dr. Lane said, smiling. "You've certainly made some amazing progress."

Paige smiled back at the distinguished-looking sixty-something-year-old man. "Yeah, I guess I have, and of course, I owe a lot of thanks to you."

"No thanks needed at all. Helping my patients is what I'm here for, and it always gives me great joy when I see success stories."

"I'm definitely better. That's for sure. But I still have a few struggles."

"When it comes to your mom, right?"

"Yes. I just don't understand why she won't have anything to do with me. Why she doesn't love her own child," Paige said, thinking back to all the therapy sessions she'd wept through due to this very thing.

"For the most part, it's because she's still in so much pain herself. And she needs someone to help her work through all of it."

"Maybe. But if you ask her, she'll swear she's fine."

Dr. Lane leaned back in his chair. "Unfortunately, she's no different than most people who have emotional problems or mental illnesses. She's no different than the thousands of folks who will never get the help they need, because in many cases, not even their family members believe they need therapy."

"Just like I didn't. And now I know that if a judge hadn't forced me to come here, I probably never would have."

"But you did, and that's what counts."

"I hope so. And at least my dad has been here for me all year long. He's been so supportive and kind, and I won't ever forget that day he told me he loved me the same as if I was his own flesh and blood and that he would never allow Mom to keep him away from me again."

"Your dad is a good man, Paige, and you're very blessed to have him in your life."

"I am, and maybe one day, through some kind of miracle, my mom will eventually love me, too."

Paige and Dr. Lane chatted for another ten minutes or so, and then Paige went back to her room to finish packing. About an hour later, Camille walked in, and oh had they come a long way. In the beginning, Camille hadn't wanted to see Paige, but as time had gone on, she'd found it in her heart to come visit her. Camille had proven she was the picture of forgiveness, and the reason Paige praised her so much was because Paige still wasn't sure she could forgive any woman who'd slept with her husband—something Pierce had admitted to Camille that morning after the motel incident—the same day they'd summoned Paige over to their home to confront her.

"You ready?" Camille said, hugging her.

"Just about. Karla should be here soon. Also, how are my niece and nephew?"

"They're fine."

"I'm glad."

There was a bit of silence, and Paige could tell that Camille knew why.

"And yes, Pierce is doing well also," Camille added.

Tears filled Paige's eyes. "I still have a hard time even saying his name to you, and I'm so sorry for what I did. I'm sorry I became so obsessed with him and tried to ruin your marriage. I know I've told you this over and over, but I hope you believe me when I say that it wasn't so much that I was in love with Pierce as it was about my jealous feelings toward you. Not to mention, I was very ill and not dealing with reality very well."

"Yes, but the past is the past, and interestingly enough, Pierce and I have never been closer. Even more so now than before all this happened. It did take some time for us to work through everything, but we have, and that's all that matters."

"Yeah, but Pierce still hates me."

"Yeah...he sort of does, and unfortunately, I think it'll be a long while before he feels any different."

"I did a lot of stuff to both of you, though, so who can blame him?"

"True, but you've been hurt, too, Paige, and that's what I finally had to think about. It's also the reason I spoke on your behalf at your trial during sentencing. Mom really has treated you badly your entire life, and it wasn't until you pointed it out to me that I took time to recognize it. I guess I saw what I wanted to see when we were kids because that's just what kids do. Then when we became adults, I just thought you and Mom were like so many other mothers and daughters I know who don't get along. But I never once stopped to wonder why, and that's where I was wrong."

"But it wasn't your fault. You never treated me terribly, but somehow in my mind I saw you as the enemy. I got things all twisted, and the next thing I knew, I made you responsible for everything. Sometimes there would even be this voice in my head, demanding that I get revenge on you, and I always felt like everyone was against me. I was paranoid all the time, and I couldn't help how I felt," Paige said, wondering why her brain didn't work the way it was supposed to. She wondered why some people were born with normal thinking while others came into the world with loads of mental issues. It was all so humiliating, but at the same time, she was glad her doctor had finally gotten to the root of her problem, delusional disorder, and found the perfect medication for her. In the beginning, he'd prescribed a few different types, searching for the right one, but it was Abilify that had finally worked. Thankfully, Paige still experienced no major side effects, and she'd been happily taking it for months.

"What are you thinking about?" Camille asked.

"This last year and how grateful I am I was able to get help."

"I'm grateful, too. Also, Paige, I hope there's one thing you'll never forget," Camille said.

"What's that?"

"That I really do love you."

"I love you, too. You're my rock, Camille, and if I have to spend the rest of my life making things up to you I will."

"You don't owe me anything. Your love is more than enough, and that's all I want from you."

Tears flowed down Paige's cheeks, and Camille hugged her again.

Paige held her sister close and thought about how blessed she was. She also thought about all the sins she'd committed, how she'd reaped all of what she had sown, and how she'd basically lost everything—her condo, her car, her PR business. But what made her smile was the fact that none of those things really mattered to her anymore, and that she was finally happy for the right reasons. She was finally living and thinking the way God wanted her to, and life was good.

But more important, she thought about the scripture Camille had told her to trust in, believe in, and the one she should recite daily: Matthew 9:22, which stated, "Daughter, be encouraged! Your faith has made you well."

God was so amazing and so very true to His Word, and Paige couldn't help smiling through all her tears. She was overjoyed and would forever be indebted—to Him and also to Camille.

She would always be thankful to both of them for their unconditional love...the one thing she'd always wanted but had never truly felt or been able to accept—until now.

READING GROUP GUIDE

Discussion Questions

1. Forgiveness is a virtue, but oftentimes, when people have hurt us, finding the strength to forgive them isn't easy. Paige's actions are cruel and destructive, yet her sister, Camille, finds it in her heart to forgive. How do you think Camille is able to do this? Is it for her benefit, Paige's, or both? If you were in a similar situation, do you think you'd be able to forgive as Camille did? Is it ever okay to put conditions on forgiveness, such as insisting a person go to counseling or stop a certain behavior in order to retain your forgiveness, or must forgiveness be unconditional?

2. While Paige's scheming pushes her sister's marriage over the edge, there are already some issues brewing between Camille and Pierce. Camille mentions that Pierce feels she is putting outside activities ahead of her family. While these activities make her happy, she considers giving them up to preserve her family. Do you think Camille is right to continue her activities outside of the home, or should she have given them up the first time Pierce mentioned it? Should Pierce be more supportive of her endeavors, or is he right to

want her at home more often? What can a woman who is a wife and mother do to find balance between her family life and her personal life?

3. Infidelity can be difficult to overcome in a marriage. Camille and Pierce are able to get past her perceived affair and his actual one; however, Andrea isn't able to forgive Derrick for his cheating. What are some of the reasons Camille and Pierce are able to stay together while Andrea and Derrick divorce? Setting aside a scheming sister-in-law manipulating the situation, is adultery ever excusable? If you were in a relationship where your partner had been unfaithful, what would you need him or her to do in order to move beyond the affair and rebuild trust?

4. Are Camille and Pierce right to keep the truth from their children early on in their separation, or should they be completely honest with them from the beginning? What are some of the ramifications that a parent's affair might have for his or her children?

5. Paige, by her own admission, uses Owen for her personal gain, but as Owen later admits, she is far from the only woman to have ever taken advantage of his generosity. Do you think Owen's reactions—first demanding Paige repay him for the money he spent on her, then telling Camille what he knows—are justified? If a woman accepts gifts or money from a man she's dating, is she under any obligation to him?

6. At the end of the story, Maxine admits she was never able to love Paige because of the circumstances under which Paige was conceived. Paige's doctor adds that because Maxine never

sought counseling after her own rape, she never dealt with the trauma, and that made her behavior toward Paige worse. Does this excuse Maxine's poor treatment of Paige? Do you think Maxine made the right choice by keeping her baby, or would Paige have been better off if Maxine had given her up for adoption? How might Paige's life have been different if she had been raised in a different home? Would she still have the same mental issues she does now, or do you think a more nurturing environment might have helped her?

7. Siblings raised in the same house can sometimes have very different experiences during childhood. For example, Paige remembers mostly hardship and anger, while Camille remembers nothing but a loving, happy family. Why do you think it was so difficult for Camille to notice what was happening to Paige when they were young? If you have siblings, can you think of any example of how your individual perceptions color the memory of an event?

Denise and Derrek Shaw have a wonderful daughter,
successful careers, a beautiful house—
and a disturbing secret...

Please turn this page
for a preview of

The Perfect Marriage.

$\mathcal{H}$i, I'm Jackson," the fifty-something man dressed in a pair of work overalls said.

"Hi, Jackson." Twenty-two men and women of various ethnic backgrounds spoke back to him in unison. They sat around three banquet-length tables that were pushed together as one, and Denise wanted to hightail it out of there as fast as she could. For nearly an hour, she and her husband, Derrek, both of them dressed in professional business suits, had listened to one recovering drug addict after another, sharing multiple horror stories; yet Denise still couldn't understand why they were there—why they were humiliating themselves in such a very shameful way. It was true that during the wee hours of the morning, Derrek had awakened from a torturous nightmare and had decided that they both needed serious help, but Denise honestly couldn't have disagreed with him more. She couldn't fathom any of his thinking because the truth of the matter was, she and Derrek weren't the least bit addicted to anything. She did take Vicodin nightly for relaxation purposes, what with all the major stress she endured as director of nursing for one of the Chicago area's largest nursing homes, but finding various ways to relax was normal for just about anyone she could think of. Then, as far as Derrek was concerned, about a year ago he'd begun snorting a little cocaine socially with a couple of his close colleagues, but that was it. Of course, he hadn't actually planned on telling Denise about his newfound indulgence but when she'd accidentally discovered a small plastic Baggie in his blazer pocket of all places, filled with some white powdery substance, she'd confronted him. He'd apologized for hiding things from her, and while she hadn't necessarily liked the idea of him using an illegal drug, she also couldn't deny that she'd always been curious about it herself. Her parents had raised her to be a "good girl," and when she'd become a teenager, they'd kept her away from "bad girl" sort of things, such as late-night parties and the kind of friends who could do whatever they wanted when they wanted to. Her father had also forbade her to be friends with any child—even her own cousins—who didn't live in a "suitable" neighborhood and didn't attend private school. He'd made it very clear that she wasn't to consort with "riffraff" of any kind unless their parents were of a certain class.

In the end, her parents had basically guarded her day and night, told her that she didn't need many friends, anyway, and insisted she should focus mainly on being the best student possible. They'd also encouraged her to read her Bible daily and had kept her frequently involved in church activities. In the end, though, this of course had all been fine because it was Denise's upbringing that had stopped her from doing anything that wasn't good for her, specifically during her college years. She hadn't even dated all that much back then and had primarily concentrated on her studies and potentially bright future in nursing. She'd learned to do exactly as her father had expected, and she'd gone very far in life because of it.

Still, for some reason, she'd always wondered what it would be like to smoke marijuana or even snort a little cocaine for that matter, simply because she'd never done anything irrational. Maybe her strong interest in trying drugs stemmed from how strict her parents had been and the fact that everything had been so off-limits. Because no matter how much education she'd gotten or how often she'd gone to church, she'd never been able to shed this relentless need to do something out of the ordinary—something wild, even. She'd known it was crazy and lowly of her to even consider such things, which was the reason she'd never shared these feelings with another living soul, but her curiosity was what it was and she couldn't help it—so much so that when the opportunity had presented itself, she'd taken it. She'd debated back and forth and then back and forth again, but three months ago when she'd found herself home alone taking a much needed day off from work, she'd pulled out Derrek's stash from the tan metal box he kept it in. Even then, as she'd held it in her hand, she'd debated a while longer but then she had finally poured a tiny line of co-caine onto one of her hand mirrors and snorted it with a straw she'd gotten from the kitchen. At first, she'd wondered how long it would take before she felt anything, but in a couple of minutes, she'd gotten her first buzz. She remembered, too, how she'd never felt more energized or stress-free in her life.

So over these last three months, she and Derrek sometimes—well, every night, that is—did a line or two in their bedroom. They only did it, though, as a way to unwind, so why not? Especially since not only was her job extremely demanding and filled with loads of responsibilities, Derrek's position as the director of finance at Covington Park Memorial Hospital was just as taxing. They both worked long hours, they did all they could trying to be the best parents they could be to their twelve-year-old daughter, Mackenzie, and at the end of every given workday a bit of cocaine always made them feel better. It took the edge off in more ways than one, but again, they weren't hooked and had not a thing to worry about.

But here the two of them were, front and center, sitting at some humdrum Narcotics Anonymous meeting among people who truly *were* addicts—folks who didn't appear to have ever lived the kind of decent life she and Derrek had worked so hard to establish. As Denise scanned the entire group one by one, she did feel sorry for these poor people, but she also couldn't help noticing that she and Derrek had nothing in common with them. Many had talked about their days of being homeless, some had mentioned not graduating from high school, and others had talked about the horrible neighborhoods they'd grown up in. Just about every single story had depressed Denise, and she wanted to leave.

So much for wishful thinking, though, because as soon as Jackson finished sharing about his last few days, Derrek spoke next.

"Hi, I'm Derrek."

"Hi, Derrek," everyone said, some smiling and some with quiet stares.

"Well, I'm not sure where to begin exactly, so I guess I'll just say that I'm very glad to be here. My wife and I," he said, looking at Denise, "have never attended any kind of meetings for addiction before, but one thing I'll never forget are the stories my grandfather told me for years about his days as an alcoholic. He would tell me how it was the worst time in his life and that had it not been for God and Alcoholics Anonymous, he would have likely been a dead man in his thirties. Before he died, he'd been sober for almost forty years, but even then, he still attended one or two meetings every week."

Many of the people around the table nodded, more of them smiling than before, and Denise hoped Derrek wasn't going to share any more of their personal business. She wondered why he couldn't handle this *so-called* drug problem in private. Some time ago, Derrek had gotten a little carried away with playing the Illinois State Lottery, but when he'd realized enough was enough, he'd prayed about it and stopped on his own. He hadn't needed any twelve-step program back then, so for the life of her, she couldn't understand why this new issue was different.

Now, instead of *hoping* he wouldn't say anything else, she wanted to *beg* him not to.

But sadly, he did.

"The real reason I wanted my wife and I to come tonight, however, is because I had this horrifying dream that scared me to death. It was very vivid and when it was all said and done, my wife and I had ended up just like my parents: strung out on drugs and living on the street. We were homeless and destitute."

Everyone stared at Derrek, attentively and compassionately, and Denise could tell their hearts went out to him—and to her, too, for that matter. The only thing was, she and Derrek *didn't* have a problem, and she wished he'd stop blowing everything out of proportion and being so dramatic.

"Anyway, I won't take up a lot of your time tonight, but again, I'm very glad to be here and thank you for having us."

"Thanks, Derrek. Keep coming back." Everyone spoke together in an almost chantlike fashion.

Derrek nodded. "I will."

Denise wanted to scream.

Two Months Later

Denise smoothed the back of her husband's head, admiring how handsome he still was, and gazed at their beautiful daughter. She honestly couldn't have been happier. They were all sitting in the family room, she and Derrek on the soft, plush, burnt orange leather sofa and Mackenzie in one of the matching oversized chairs. Mackenzie's long, slender legs were also propped up on one of the ottomans as she sipped strawberry soda from an ice-filled glass. Tonight was pizza night and, while Denise hadn't eaten any, Mackenzie and her father had devoured as much as they could. They were also in the midst of watching *The Color Purple* for the umpteenth time and were enjoying every minute of it.

But as Denise glanced over at Derrek again, she thought about how blessed they truly were. They'd been married for fifteen wonderful years, she still loved him more than ever, and he clearly felt the same about her. She knew there was no such thing as a perfect marriage, but if there had been, her marriage to Derrek would certainly have to qualify; partly because they undoubtedly had the love of a lifetime and partly because no disagreement or problem had ever come between them. Then if that wasn't enough, God had blessed them with the best daughter. She was kind and smart, she loved everyone she came in contact with, and she never got into trouble. She also had a knack for helping any of her school-mates who were a lot less fortunate whenever they were in need of something. She'd been gifted with an old soul for sure, and she was the kind of child any parent could be proud of.

Then, in addition to their marriage and daughter, God had given them both successful careers. They'd each graduated from top schools, she from Johns Hopkins University with a bachelor's degree in nursing and then a master's in nursing from the University of Illinois at Chicago and Derrek from Northwestern with a bachelor's in business and then an MBA from the same grad school as her. Denise had gone to college on a partial academic scholarship, but it also hadn't been a problem for her parents to cover the balance of her tuition since her father had been a top criminal attorney in downtown Chicago for years. Derrek, on the other hand, hadn't come from a well-to-do family and had been forced to struggle and work his way through school. He'd also had to utilize as many grants and student loans that had been available to him. As a matter of fact, because Derrek's parents had gotten so caught up with drugs, it had been his maternal grandparents who had raised him and his twin brother, Dixon. Neither of his grandparents had earned huge salaries, but they'd still given their two grandsons a good home and had done the best they could with them.

When Denise heard Shug Avery saying, "I's married now," she gazed at the large flat-screen television and thought about her own wedding. The ceremony had been amazing, and she still remembered every detail as if it was yesterday. Eight bridesmaids, eight groomsmen, two maids of honor, two best men, three gorgeous little flower girls, the most handsome little ring bearer, and nearly five hundred guests. It had all been a dream come true for both Denise and Derrek, and their family members had been just as happy. In fact, life had been good since the very first day they'd met, which had sort of happened by accident. Right after completing her nursing program, Denise had immediately gotten hired by Covington Park Memorial, and as it had turned out, Derrek had started working for the hospital's finance department the same week. But the reason she'd always felt their meeting had been by accident was because she'd received employment offers from two other hospitals in the Chicago area, and it hadn't been until a couple of days before her scheduled hire date that she'd decided against one of them and had checked to see if the offer was still on the table from Covington. She'd changed her mind at the last minute for no particular reason, although her mom always insisted that there were no such things as accidents or coincidences, only meant-to-be situations. Her mom believed that everything truly did happen for a reason.

Derrek laughed at one of the funnier scenes in the movie and grabbed Denise's hand. The romance between them was still very much alive, and she couldn't be more grateful. The only thing was, however, suddenly, she felt somewhat out of sorts and a bit uneasy. She knew why, though: she'd had another long, hectic day at work, and she needed something to calm her nerves. Nothing major, but just a little something to help her through the rest of the evening and prepare her for a restful night of sleep. But just as she started to get up, Mackenzie said, "Oh, Mom and Dad, I forgot to tell you. Alexis's parents are leaving two days earlier than we are for their Christmas trip, so is it okay for her to stay here with us?"

"Of course," Denise said. "She's going to be traveling with us for the holidays, anyway."

"I told her you wouldn't mind, but she still wanted me to ask. I think her mom is going to call you, too."

"It's no problem at all."

"Gosh, only three more months." Mackenzie beamed. "Jamaica is gonna be so much fun, and I'm so glad Alexis is going. We're gonna have an even better time than we had on the cruise last year."

"I'm excited, too," Denise said just before Mackenzie's phone rang.

Derrek pressed the PAUSE button on the DVR, and Mackenzie checked her caller ID screen.

"This is Alexis now. I'll call her back, though, when the movie goes off."

"You sure?" he asked.

"Uh-huh."

Derrek pressed the PLAY button, and Denise scooted toward the edge of the sofa. "I need to review a couple of care plan files for tomorrow, but I'll be back down in a half hour or so."

Mackenzie looked at her mother. "But, Mom, you're gonna miss the rest of the movie."

"Well, maybe not all of it. I'll try to finish up as soon as I can."

Mackenzie didn't say anything else and turned back toward the television. Derrek did the same, and Denise strolled through the hallway and up the wooden, carpeted, winding staircase. They'd lived in this particular house for only five years, but it was their dream home. They'd owned two houses prior to this, first their starter home, which had been fifteen hundred square feet, then their second, which was nearly double that size, and now this one, which was right at five thousand. There were three finished levels that included four bedrooms, a theater room, an exercise room, and three fireplaces. They'd built it brand new, so not only was this their third home, it was their last. This was the house they would retire in and the one they would eventually sell many years from now when they were too old and too tired to worry about normal upkeep. They would then happily and readily scale down to a nice little condo.

Denise stepped inside her bedroom, closed the door, and hurried over to her handbag. She'd gone all day without taking anything, but now her stress level was getting the best of her. So she unzipped the middle compartment, pulled out an unlabeled bottle, and opened it. She tapped it with her left forefinger until one large, white, oblong-shaped pill fell into her hand. Then, she went into the bathroom and turned on the faucet. She wasn't too keen on drinking from the tap, mainly because she was so used to drinking bottled water, but she knew tap would have to do because she didn't want to traipse all the way back downstairs to the kitchen and take a chance on Derrek seeing her and questioning what she was doing.

She ran the water for sixty seconds or so, waiting for it to cool down, and then she lifted a decorative cup from the top of the vanity. When it was half full, she tossed the Vicodin into her mouth, gulped down some water, and swallowed. She immediately drank the rest of it, went back into the bedroom, and sat in one of the high-back chairs in the sitting area.

Then she waited. She did this because she knew her body would be relaxed in no time. She'd been pretty hungry when she'd first gotten home, but the reason she hadn't eaten pizza with Derrek and Mackenzie was because a few months ago, she'd learned that when she took Vicodin on an empty stomach, the euphoria was much more intense and it gave her a warm feeling. It also took only thirty minutes or less to take full effect, and this was the reason she'd had no choice but to lie to her daughter about having to go upstairs to work. She hated being dishonest, but she'd needed an excuse to get away for at least forty-five minutes to an hour so she could enjoy the way the Vicodin made her feel. She would also take another before going to bed. Not because she needed to, but because she wanted to. She knew Derrek wouldn't agree and wouldn't understand but no matter what he said, she saw nothing inappropriate about feeling good. She also knew he'd be livid if he somehow discovered that she hadn't fully given up cocaine either or that she'd secretly found her own dealer to buy from. Derrek was still dead set on going to those Narcotics Anonymous meetings every now and then, meaning he hadn't done any cocaine ever since that first gathering he'd dragged her along to, but Denise hadn't gone back. She also knew Derrek wouldn't be happy if he found out she still *did* snort cocaine from time to time and that she now took Vicodin on a pretty regular basis—even though the pain in her hip, which resulted from her falling on a sheet of ice, had vanished months ago. He'd be terribly disappointed if he ever learned that her orthopedic specialist hadn't written her a prescription for Vicodin ever since— he would certainly hit the roof if he somehow discovered that she now got her pills any way she could; at first from doctor friends, who hadn't seemed to mind writing her a prescription, but when they'd eventually stopped taking her calls, she'd begun buying them from the same guy who sold her cocaine. Actually, it was a good thing she was the one who handled their family finances because it was for this reason that Derrek hadn't noticed the extra money she was spending.

But no matter how Denise looked at things, she saw nothing wrong with any of what she was doing. Not when she clearly had total control and wasn't addicted to anything. Still, she would keep her Vicodin and cocaine moments to herself. She decided that silence was best for everyone involved.

Derrek repositioned his tie in front of the dresser mirror, making sure it wasn't crooked, and the home phone rang. It was pretty early on a Friday morning for anyone to be calling, but when he stepped closer to the phone sitting on the nightstand and saw that it was his brother, Dixon, he rolled his eyes and ignored it. He was glad that even though a lot of time had passed, Dixon still had the same cell number because had he changed it, Derrek might have thought someone else was calling, and he could have made the mistake of answering.

"Who's that?" Denise asked.

"Nobody."

Denise shook her head, slipped on one of her hoop earrings and snapped it closed. "So, honey, exactly how long are you planning to go without speaking to your brother? It's been at least three years now."

"Yeah, and I still don't have a thing to say to him."

Just thinking about the way Dixon had treated him was enough to piss Derrek off. Derrek had done everything for his brother—his twin brother at that—but all Dixon had done was lie, tell more lies, and use Derrek every chance he got. He was outrageously selfish and while Derrek had allowed Dixon to borrow money multiple times, promise to pay it back, and never make good on it, the stunt he'd pulled three years ago had been too much.

For years, Derrek had loaned Dixon two hundred here and five hundred there, but with this last occurrence, Dixon had called him up claiming he'd been laid off from his job and that he needed five thousand dollars to cover his bills: mortgage, car note, utilities, and a few medical expenses. Derrek had known it was a lot of money to be loaning anyone, even his own brother, but after he and Denise had discussed it and Dixon had sworn he would pay them back just as soon as he borrowed money from his retirement account, Derrek had gone to the bank and gotten a cashier's check. Dixon had thanked him profusely and promised again that he would repay the money in a couple of weeks or so. Sadly, a couple of weeks had come and gone and by the time a full month had passed, Derrek had learned from a mutual friend that Dixon had taken his girlfriend on a ten-day trip to Paris.

Derrek hadn't wanted to believe his own flesh and blood would deceive him this way, but sure enough, when he'd called Dixon and questioned him about the money, Dixon had stuttered between words but then flat out told Derrek, "I don't have it." Then, when Derrek had asked him about the trip, Dixon had said, "Look, man...okay, yeah, it's true. I took my girl on a nice vacation just like you do every year with Denise. So why don't you stop badgering me about that funky little five thousand dollars. It's not like you need it right back anyhow." Derrek remembered how he'd almost cracked up laughing at his brother because surely he couldn't have been serious. Surely he hadn't meant a word he'd just said and had only been joking. But after thirty seconds of total silence, Derrek quickly realized his brother *had* meant every word he'd said, and Derrek hadn't spoken to Dixon ever since.

"Honey, are you listening to me?" Derrek heard Denise saying.

"I'm sorry, baby; I guess I was somewhere else."

Denise ran a brush through her bouncy, black, shoulder-length hair and moved closer to him. "You were thinking about your brother, weren't you?"

"Yeah, but not anymore."

"Honey, I really wish you would talk to Dixon. Listen to what he has to say and then just forgive him. Life is way too short for this."

"Dixon should have thought about that three years ago."

Denise set the brush on the dresser and held Derrek's hands. "I understand how you feel, but baby, he made a mistake. And it was a long time ago."

Derrek gazed at her with sad eyes. "I appreciate what you're trying to do, but as far as I'm concerned, I don't even have a brother."

Denise walked back over to the bed and placed a few items in her purse. Derrek could tell she wasn't happy with his response, but he couldn't help the way he felt. A part of him wished he could let bygones be bygones because sometimes he truly missed his brother, but for some reason he just couldn't. Not this time. Not when his brother had totally disrespected him and acted as though what he'd done was no big deal. Not when his brother had hurt him to the core, knowing full well that the two of them had already suffered more than enough during childhood. In fact, their mother and father had left both of them with such painful memories, Derrek still hadn't forgiven them, either. How could he? How could anyone forgive a mother and a father who could so easily choose drugs over their own children? Leave two eight-year-old little boys home alone for days without food or clean clothing?

How could Derrek forgive any adult who could be so awful to any human being?

That had been almost thirty years ago, but sometimes the mere thought of his parents and what they'd done to him and Dixon brought Derrek to tears. After all this time, he still hadn't gotten completely over his childhood and wondered if he ever would.

There was something great that had resulted from it all, though: his grandparents. They'd both passed away a few years back, but he thanked God for them because had they not taken him and Dixon to live with them, he wasn't sure how their lives might have turned out.

His childhood woes were also the reason he'd sworn he'd never be anything like his parents—the reason he loved, honored, and cherished his gorgeous wife, the reason having a close relationship with his daughter was so important. It was also because of his parents that he'd vowed to never do drugs under any circumstances. To his great disappointment, though, he'd resorted to using cocaine. He hadn't planned on doing it, but one day he'd gone to the home of one of his colleagues to watch a football game and the next thing he'd known, one of the guys had passed him a line and he'd taken a hit.

It had been the stupidest thing in the world for him to do, but it also hadn't taken him long to realize how much he liked it. He'd loved how calm it made him feel and how the emotional stress he'd struggled with since that morning hadn't mattered to him for the rest of that evening.

To this day, he still hadn't told Denise what had triggered his decision to try cocaine for the first time because he hadn't wanted to upset her—and he never would tell her—but earlier that day he'd been told he might have cancer. His doctor had run a couple of scans on what had seemed like some sort of small, malignant tumor in his groin area, but once the growth had been removed

and a biopsy had been performed, Derrek had learned it was be-
nign. He hadn't been told the final results, though, until a couple
of days after his initial scare, and by then, Derrek had snorted cocaine three evenings straight. He hadn't wanted to stop, and for
the rest of the week, he'd simply told Denise that he'd been working late. Ironically, she actually *had* been working longer hours
than usual, so with her being much too tired for sex for a period
of days, she'd never even noticed his scar.

Thankfully, though, that terrifying dream he'd had two
months ago had made him think long and hard, and he was glad
he'd come to his senses—glad he'd realized that he and Denise
had begun loving cocaine just a bit too much and that he'd suggested they go to a Narcotics Anonymous meeting. No, they
hadn't lost their jobs, cleaned out their savings accounts, nor were
they living on the street, but just knowing that he and Denise had
begun snorting lines together every evening had made him think.
It was true that maybe his insisting that they attend a meeting
centered on a twelve-step program was a bit over the top, but
nonetheless, it had stopped them both from getting high and he
was happy about that.

After Derrek slipped on his shoes and tied them, he grabbed
his blazer. Denise slid on her watch and snapped the clasp shut,
and they headed downstairs. Mackenzie was already parked at the
granite-top island eating a bowl of cereal and reading one of her
textbooks, and Denise went over to the coffeepot. For years she'd
been adding fresh coffee grounds to the filter each night before
going to bed, so all she did now was press the START button.

"Sweetie, you have debate practice after school today, right?"
Denise asked Mackenzie, because on those days, Mackenzie
couldn't take the bus home or carpool with her friends who had
stay-at-home moms. Either Derrek or Denise had to pick her up.

"Yep. Oh, and we're staying an extra two hours tonight. Mr.

Braxton says we need to put in a little more time this week, so we'll be ready for the competition next Thursday."

"So is the topic still about K–12 students in the state of Illinois and whether they should attend school year-round?"

"Yep. And while I don't necessarily think it would be good for any of us to go without a summer break, I'm sort of glad our team will be showing the benefits of it. There's so much information out there to support that particular aspect of the argument."

Denise smiled. "I'm so glad you joined the debate team. I loved being on debate when I was in school because we learned so much about controversial topics."

Derrek placed two slices of bread in the toaster. "I loved being on the team, too, when I was your age. I was also on the high school team all four years," he said, looking over at the ringing phone. It was Dixon again, and Derrek pretended not to hear it. "So when is the actual debate?"

Mackenzie watched him move to the other side of the kitchen. "Daddy, is that Uncle Dixon calling?"

"Unfortunately, it is, sweetie."

"Well, Daddy, why won't you talk to him? And why can't I see him anymore?"

"I'm sorry things aren't good between my brother and me, but you'll understand when you're older. Plus, if your uncle really wanted to talk to us or even apologize, he'd leave a message."

Mackenzie lowered her eyes. "Maybe he's afraid to."

Derrek didn't say anything.

Still she continued. "Daddy, I think you're wrong to treat Uncle Dixon like this, because by now, I'm sure even God has forgiven him for whatever he did."

Denise finally chimed in, and Derrek was surprised she hadn't done so before now. "Sweetie, you're right," she said. "God forgives us for everything. All we have to do is ask Him."

Two against one. Derrek knew there was no way to win this conversation, so he flipped the television on and turned it to CNN. He watched Soledad O'Brien, Roland Martin, and two other popular political analysts for a few minutes, but once the coffee was ready, he drank a cup, ate his toast, and grabbed his briefcase. But the phone rang again.

Denise walked over to it. "Baby, why don't you at least see what your brother wants? He's made a lot of calls over the last few days. For at least a week now."

Derrek did something that was rare for him: he blatantly ignored his wife's comment. "Mackenzie, if you're ready, we'd better get going. Unless you want to take the bus." He always teased his daughter every chance he got about getting rides versus riding the bus, but today he did it as a way to change the subject.

Denise folded her arms, though, clearly aware of what he was up to.

"I'm sorry," he said, walking over and kissing her on the lips.

"I just wish you'd rethink your position on this."

"I love you," he said. "And I'll see you later."

Derrek kissed her again and walked out to the garage. He wished he could feel differently but if his brother didn't stop calling, Derrek would contact the phone company and have his number blocked. He would do whatever he had to to get rid of him.